Samru the Fearless Warrior

Samru the Fearless Warrior

A historical novel

Jaipal Singh

Srishti
PUBLISHERS & DISTRIBUTORS

Srishti Publishers & Distributors
Registered Office: N-16, C.R. Park
New Delhi – 110 019
Corporate Office: 212A, Peacock Lane
Shahpur Jat, New Delhi – 110 049
editorial@srishtipublishers.com

First published by SRISHTI PUBLISHERS & DISTRIBUTORS in 2004
Copyright © Jaipal Singh 2004

ISBN 9788188575213

Typeset in AGaramond 11pt. by Suresh Kumar Sharma at Srishti

Cover design by Creative Concept

Contents

The Author

Jaipl Singh was born in Solan in Himachal Pradesh. He had his education in Lahore and later at Glasgow University. He has been interested in freelance writing from his student days and has written articles and essays on variety of subjects.

He has published two collections of short stories 'Nainha Khan & other stories' and 'The Ragpicker & other stories.'

Acknowledgements

For collecting material for this work, I visited different libraries and made notes from original sources that could be located and then used the information for my initial drafts of the subject on the computer. Because of my clumsy handling of the computer I often found myself in frustrating situations when I thought that I had lost the work of months. Whenever this or some other seeming disaster happened, my grandson Ishaan came to my rescue in retrieving written material. I owe a lot of gratitude of him.

My other family members specially Rachna and Nomita were a great support for the publication of the book. My wife Toshi made valuable suggestions.

I am indebted to my publisher, for the friendly interest he took in the manuscript and its publication.

Haveli

Dark clouds loomed large in the sky as Gulbadan Jaan stepped out of her palanquin. It was like the gloom in her mind, unsure, intense, overwhelming. She sighed deeply in an attempt to lighten her heart, wishing the strong winds would blow away the impending rain.

Salamat, her friend of many years would be able to help her out, she hoped. Gulbadan's fortunes were fast declining. She was in dire financial crisis, and who else could she turn to for advice but Salamat Jaan who herself had seen difficult days. Salamat Jaan was many years older to her and had shut down her establishment many years ago, when she felt that she was too old to carry on in the profession.

But, Salamat Jaan could not offer her a solution rightaway. She said.

"Look, I cannot think of anything now. I am going to Faizabad in Awadh, to see Pyaro Bai. She has invited me to stay with her for sometime. You might remember her. She was one of the rising stars of my *kotha,* before I shut it down.

She had migrated to Faizabad, when going had become tough for me. Let me find out how she is doing. I will suggest a way out when I come back to Delhi."

Rather dejected, Gulbadan started back for her home.

As her curtained palanquin approached the massive steps of Shah Jahan's Jama Masjid in Delhi, she heard the heart-rending cries of a girl.

"Hai ! Hai ! my Amma is dying."

She parted the curtains of the palanquin a little and peerd out. A woman was lying on the step of a mosque and a girl, about eight years old, was crying by her side. Gulbadan noticed within a fleeting second that the girl, though dirty with unkempt hair and soiled face had lovely expressive eyes.

The palanquin was lowered and Gulbadan in her *burqa* stepped out, and walked towards the girl. As she approached them, the wails became louder.

"Please help me, I do not know where to go or what to do."

The woman lying on the step turned and looked up at Gulbadan. She had a faint feeling that she had seen this woman earlier somewhere, but could not recollect who she was. She asked through her veil:

"Where do you want to go?"

"To the *haveli* of Gulbadan Jaan, the famous courtesan."

Gulbadan was taken aback but did not reveal her identity.

"What is your name?" she asked.

"Jaddan."

The name struck a chord in her memory, and Gulbadan asked again:

"Why do you want to go to her place?"

"That is the only place where I spent many happy years of my unfortunate life." The woman sobbed.

Gulbadan hired a *palki*, and asked the child and the mother to get into it.

"You are not well. We will talk at leisure once you become all right."

As they arrived outside the house, Jaddan could make out even in her distraught state that the *haveli's* exterior was in a shabby state, with the stucco cracking in different places, and even falling from many points.

They entered the *deorhi*, and the little girl was awestruck with the colonnaded corridors running alongside on both right and left of a massive courtyard. In front there was a massive deep pavilion like verandah, with living rooms along its back. There were some rooms along its side too. The courtyard was divided into floored terraces, at three different levels, with the lowest terrace at the entrance, just next to the lobby. In a corner of the lowest terrace there was a well.

The mother and the child were put up in a room. A female retainer of Gulbadan Jaan brought them food. An elderly Hakim was called in, who prescribed medicines and herbal tonics for Jaddan. The female retainer then washed the girl, and brought a set of clean clothes for her.

When Gulbadan saw the girl after her bath, she immediately realised that she would be a great asset to her kotha in the years to come. She was quite a connoisseur in spotting the potential in pretty girls. It was an essential pre-requisite in her profession. Gulbadan asked the girl her name.

"Farzana."

"I will call you Farzo." Gulbadan said.

Memories flooded Gulbadan's mind. More than twenty years ago she too had stepped into this haveli as a young girl. It was the day following the Eid-ul-Zuha when Nadir Shah, the Iranian invader who had defeated the army of the Mughal Emperor of Delhi, had personally moved towards Chandni Chowk, the central market, mounted on a magnificent horse. It had been reported to him that many of his soldiers had been killed during the night by rioting mobs, after a rumour had been circulated that he had been poisoned to death. He had decided to suppress the riot. A musket shot was aimed at him, which killed one of his officers by his side. This so incensed him that he ordered a general plunder and mass slaughter of the inhabitants of Delhi. They were ordered to burn the houses of the natives.

Gulbadan was about six years old then. When the invader's soldiers started burning down the houses in their neighbourhood, her father and mother ran out holding her hand. Her father was a wellknown Jyotishi (astrologer)

4

patronised by the nobility and the businessmen. Mughal Emperor Mohammed Shah himself used to consult him at times. The soldiers spotted them, and speared the man to death. They pushed Gulbadan's mother into a corner under the watchful eyes of some soldiers where a few other women too were held captive. Her father's horrendous dying shriek left a lasting impression on the child's memory and she remembered every aspect of her life thereafter. In panic, the child started running towards a narrow lane in the opposite direction. She ran into an elderly man with a long flowing snowy-white beard. He picked her up and hurriedly took her to the haveli of Nur Bai, the famous courtesan. Nur Bai was always looking for little girls who would brighten up the future of her kotha. He said to Nur Bai.

"Her father has been killed and mother captured. He was a Hindu astrologer. You can bring her up as a Hindu or convert her, as you like it."

"There is no religion in our profession. Looking at her I can vouch for it that she would grow up to be a beautiful woman. We shall train her and God willing, she would become a successful courtesan."

She gave two gold pieces to the old man.

After a few days Jaddan recovered, and went to thank Gulbadan Jaan. She was still worried; she didn't know whether she would be allowed to continue in the *haveli*. If not, where would she go with a little girl in tow! Gulbadan's words, however, reassured her.

"Jaddo, I can see that you are apprehensive about your future. But don't worry, you can live with us here, and we shall teach your daughter to read and write Urdu. Allah willing, she would be able to recite Urdu poetry of eminent poets like Mir Taki Mir and Sauda. She may even be able to compose her own couplets in years to come. I see a very bright future for her as a courtesan. She may rival the success of my benefactor Nur Bai. May peace be upon her soul! If she is keen, she can learn Farsi, so that she can converse with the nobility in that language. Then, she would not be considered a mere nautch girl, she would gain respect and high regard."

"*Chaudhrayan!* I am indeed very lucky to have met you. You have been very kind to my daughter and me. May Allah bless you with all the happiness!"

Kotha

Jaddan assumed charge of kitchen and was soon involved with the routine chores of the *haveli*. Earlier, she remembered, they had to feed some twenty people. She was surprised that the number had dwindled to just six. There were practically no *mujras* in the *haveli*. She recalled during her earlier stay, the Haveli known as *mehfil* saw hectic activity with *kathak* dances, classical music and poetry recitations. On important occasions Gulbadan Jaan herself presented mujras.

Patrons of the *mehfil* were rich and important *umara* of the Mughal court, and were great admirers of Gulbadan Jaan. She was a very pretty woman in her younger days, elegance adorning every graceful movement of her body. The patrons arrived on heavily caparisoned elephants, or sturdy Arab horses, attired in silk and loaded with jewellery and pearls. On certain occasions such as marriages and birthdays, Gulbadan Jaan was invited over with her team of dancers, singers and instrumentalists. Gifts would be sent in advance to the haveli. Jaddan was not a good dancer but she used to accompany Gulbadan when she had performances outside the haveli.

Once, Jaddan could see a very strange spectacle. Ameer Begum, another wellknown *nautch* girl too had been invited to perform in a house. She came to the function with tattoos on her breasts in the shape of a bodice, and tattoos on her legs that appeared as if she had a pair of trousers on. Only those who knew it could make out that she wore no clothes. Both the leading dancers chanted *ghazals* and poetry and danced with perfect grace. Jaddan still remembered the Urdu couplets Gulbadan recited.

> *Aag thai ibtadai ishq mein hum*
> *Ab jo hain khak inteha hai yeh*
>
> *I was all fire when first I fell in love;*
> *Now at the last, nothing but ash remains.*
>
> *This was greeted with shouts of* 'hai! hai!'.

'But why do you worry? We are still there,' some others said. Numerous gifts of gold were showered on Gulbadan, and her eyes glistened with tears. Moved by the applause and appreciation, she recited another couplet.

> *Mohabbat na ho kaash makhlook ko*
> *Na chodai yeh aashiq na mashook ko*

Would that mankind were immune to love,

For it spares neither lover nor beloved.

Everyone stood up with shouts of Wah! Wah! Some nobles went up to her to present gifts of gold.

After this, Jaddan always wanted to enquire about this secret love of hers but could not muster enough courage. But that time was long past.

One day finding Gulbadan in a quiet and pensive mood, Jaddan went to her:

"*Chaudhrayan*, is something worrying you?"

"Yes Jaddo, my income has dropped drastically. You must have noticed the shabby state of this *haveli*, which had seen prosperous days, and its magnificence was unmatched in the time of Nur Bai. Now we don't have many patrons and they are not of the class who visited us earlier." Gulbadan lamented.

"But why does this happen?"

"Jaddo you don't realise, our profession depends on the wealth of our patrons. After the destruction and havoc wrought by the Marathas, Nadir Shah ravished this city, and took away every thing he could lay his hands on, whether the diamond of Kohi Noor, the peacock throne of Shah Jahan, gold or women. In fact, Nadir Shah plundered the entire wealth accumulated in the previous two hundred years by the Mughal Emperors. They did not even spare young boys. Our Emperor was so weak he could not provide any protection to anybody. Law and order broke down completely; criminals and robbers, made life difficult for the citizens. People with means felt so insecure that large number of rich nobles and businessmen migrated to Faizabad where the Nawab of Awadh held his court. Awadh grew in wealth and importance. Many establishments of our profession also moved over to Faizabad and apparently are doing very well.'

"You have not considered shifting there yourself?"

"Never! I am too attached to this haveli.'

Jaddan had only heard about Nur Bai. She was curious to know more.

"Tell me about Nur Bai. How did she train you?"

"She gave me this name – Gulbadan. There were numerous young girls in the haveli, though may be I was the youngest. We all grew up under the strict gaze of Nur Bai. In course of time, she grew very fond of me. She had a couple of eunuchs, who used to guard the dancers and young girls in this *haveli*. For about three years I had rigorous education in Urdu and Farsi languages. She was particular that I must learn to recite Urdu poetry. That was the era when there was an efflorescence of Urdu poetry and the nobility and the rich people patronised the Urdu poets. I had a natural liking for *ghazals* and as I grew up, I became a great admirer of the poetry of Mir Taki Mir and of Mirza Muhammad Rafi Sauda, the then popular poets of Delhi. I could recite their ghazals from memory, which absolutely amazed Nur Bai and she would often say that she was more than convinced that I was the daughter of a Brahman couple. According to her, only a Brahman child could be that intelligent.

My old Ustad told Nur Bai that I was very talented and he thought I should learn Hindustani classical music. She herself was an accompalished singer of classical *raagas*. She was particularly fond of *raagas Todi and Darbari* and was much in demand as a singer. The Ustad introduced me to *khayal*, a classical form of music, which had been popular a few decades before. I also learnt other *raagas* and had to practise regularly and intensively, as my teacher was a hard taskmaster.

Thus, my training in Kathak dances, music and even styles of coquetry, were taken up in right earnest under the direct supervision of Nur Bai. She pampered me so much, that I worshipped the very ground where she walked. She would often make me sleep with her, and hug me tightly. She would kiss me on the cheeks and lips. Later I learnt that she was a *chapti* and that she often used to invite one of the pretty girls of her establishment to sleep with her."

Gulbadan was swept over by the current of memories. Her face lit up, and her voice quivered with emotion.

"Jaddan, those who had not actually set eyes on her could never imagine how pretty she was. I used to gaze at her and she would laugh seeing this. The gloss of youth in her hair and her marble like skin, mouth, eyebrows, eyelashes all looked pristine and fresh, as in the day they were created by Allah. Her figure was perfection personified, her throat was like a tower of ivory, her eyes that of a gazelle. It was no wonder that she was the rage of Hindustan. People used to say that she was fit to be the

11

Empress of India. She was an excellent conversationalist and had the gift of gab and repartee. Audience went into raptures listening to her commentaries. She was quite imperious in her behaviour, her patrons showered so much wealth on her that she was said to be richer than the Queen of the Mughal Emperor."

Gaddan stopped for a while and looked around.

"She built this *haveli* to keep up with the richest nobles of the Kingdom, and the interior was furnished with costly Persian carpets and fancy chandeliers. In the hall as well as in the top tier terrace of the courtyard four *takhats* (wooden platforms) were put together with cotton mats over them. Above the *takhats* in the courtyard there was a colourful awning. They were covered with white stretched sheets with no sign of crease. In the main bedroom there was an elegant beautiful bed with four slender and very soft oblong pillows. The pillows were placed one on top of the other. On top of these were two tiny 'flower pillows' which supported her cheeks on either side when she lay down. Lower down on each side of the bed were two small round cushions, which supported the thighs. On a *takhat* in front of the bed, a carpet was spread to mark the seat of honour. On this carpet and touching the bed was a *gau*, a large barrel shaped cushion. She had numerous palanquins with different coloured silk curtains. She went around in aristocratic style and was preceded and followed by armed retainers."

"Were there other popular dancing girls in her time?" Jaddan wanted to know.

"Oh! yes. Next in fame and importance was Saras Roop. Once a person saw her, he would keep looking at her. She was an elegant dancer. Her singing was like a whiff of breeze from heaven. It was not easy to meet her. One had to have an introduction and she had to be given a substantial advance. Chimni too was very popular, though essentially as a singer. She was a great favourite of Emperor Mohammed Shah. He used to invite her frequently to the Red Fort to sing for him. I had met her once, and remember that she had a pleasant demeanor. Then, there was Gulab whose songs made the listeners swoon, her coquettry intoxicated men. She had a telling gift of repartee, which hugely amused her fans. There was Tanno who was a great favourite of the Emperor in her younger days for her beautiful well-proportioned body and sweet and delicate voice. During her performance she used to indulge in lot of banter using swear words, which became her trademark. There were numerous other singers specialising in *raag khyal* and other forms of classical music."

"Were there any other dancers or singers as wealthy as Nur Bai?"

"No! No! No one else was any where near her in popularity or wealth." Gulbadan said. "Nur Bai was extremely demanding. Rich people, who visited her *haveli* regularly, were ruined in course of time. People said she sucked wealth out of people, the way leech sucks blood. But I must say she was very kind to me, well, most of the times. I saw her harsh face only once"

Gulbadan's face wore a faraway look and Jaddo thought that her eyes glistened.

"One of the young nobles, who visited the mehfil frequently, became my ardent admirer and I too took a fancy to him. We used to exchange glances and during *mujras*, I used to go up to him and make a low bow. Nur Bai with her hawk like eyes noticed our mutual admiration for each other. Once when the dance was over, the young noble followed me. Nur Bai blocked his path and yelled.

'Keep off her, and don't ever visit my mehfil. If you dare to come here, I will have you thrown out.'

She asked me to go with her to her room. Her voice was very grave when she started speaking.

'Look Gulbadan, in our profession there is no place for permanent affection. Whenever we wish to ensnare anyone we pretend to fall in love with him. With the art of coquetry. We can virtually make him fall on our feet and exploit him for our maximum advantage till our full. But there shouldn't be any lasting relationship with anyone. You forget about that noble.'

I burst into tears and told her that I was really in love with him and would like to live with him; he had already expressed his desire to marry me. Nur Bai was furious at me and gave me a tight slap. I ran crying to my room. I was so upset that I refused to dance for one week. I begged her again and again to let me get married but she was very firm and became more annoyed with me."

"Nur Bai was so insensitive."

"No, Jaddan, when I think about it now, I feel she had no choice if she was to be successful. Popular dancers cannot be allowed to leave because they are much in demand for marriages. We age very fast and we have to make the best of our young age.

You too might think me cruel, the manner I passed you on to a Sayyad who promised to marry you. I had to part with you, you could not have flourished in the haveli, you were not a good dancer or singer."

Salamat Jaan dropped in just then, quite unexpectedly. "*Arrey!* What are you gossiping about?"

Gulbadan was happy to see her friend. "I was telling her about Nur Bai."

Salamat Jaan was also a well-known dancer during the times when Nur Bai held the Delhi nobility enthralled. Jaddan went away leaving the friends alone to reminisce about their past.

"Talking of Nur Bai, I wonder if you have ever heard of the Hindu businessman, Chunna Mal. You must have been pretty small then." Salamat said.

"No, I don't remember him."

"Chunna Mal was a very successful jeweller who supplied

pearls, diamonds, rubies and gold ornaments to the nobility and even the Mughal Queen and the Emperor. He was rolling in wealth but he had no children. His wife too died suddenly leaving the old man all alone. To amuse himself, he started frequenting the *mujras* at Nur Bai's *haveli*. As time passed, a peculiar obsession began to eat into him. He asked for a favour from Nur Bai – each day, he wanted to spend some time all alone with her.

'You senile fool, have you gone out of your mind?' shrieked Nur Bai.

'Oh don't misunderstand me, I just want to hold your hands and sit looking at you.'

'I am sure you can do no harm but this favour would prove very expensive.'

Nur Bai demanded a huge sum for each exclusive visit. She herself had told me about this. People say that by the time Chunna Mal died, most of his wealth had passed on to Nur Bai."

Salamat continued.

"Ah, yes! As I had told you I went to Faizabad and stayed with Pyaro for about a month. I found out that she was a great favourite of Nawab Shuja ud Daula. When he went on his travels in his kingdom, Pyaro accompanied his caravan in a separate bullock cart, with her tents of stately grandeur in carts, along-with those of the Nawab; all were guarded by a party of about ten soldiers. She holds great sway over the Nawab, she has even helped a few to get important jobs in the kingdom. It is said that Hakim Mahdi was appointed the Governor of a province of Awadh on her intervention.

Shuja by nature is said to be fascinated by beautiful women, and is fond of dancing and singing. There is such a multitude of bazaar beauties and dancers in the town that no lane or alley is without them. Nawab's patronization has made them so immensely wealthy that most of the courtesans have two or three tents attached to their houses. Pyaro's house is magnificent though not as big as your *haveli*.

I tell you it would be best for you to shift to Faizabad. You are still young and very pretty. Take Farzana with you, I am sure you will make a fortune. Faizabad court is very kind to all those who are the votaries of fine arts. Musicians throng the place. Urdu poets from Hyderabad, Agra and Delhi receive tremendous support and encouragement, many have permanently settled there. Even Mir Hassan and Nazir have made Faizabad their abode. As far as dancing is concerned, the Nawab is crazy about it."

"It is very kind of you to say that I am still pretty. But, what do I do with this *haveli*?"

"Sell it."

"Who will buy it? The area is known as t*awaif*'s neighbourhood. The so-called respectable businessmen, who patronize us, look down on us. They will never buy any property in our area. These people are a hypocritical lot. No one else has any money. And then, for how long will I be able to work? And, I think you are overestimating Farzana. She has not been able to pick up the finer nuances of singing or dancing; of course, I am still trying to train her. But yes, she has turned out to be beautiful and charming."

Salamat nodded in agreement. She said.

"In Faizabad I learnt that many noble men prefer young boys to girls. Even the Mughal Emperor Mahommed Shah, it seems, would rather have boys. There are a few establishments, which cater to their tastes. In fact, Pyaro suggested that you may consider keeping boys too."

"Somebody made this suggestion during Nur Bai's time as well. She was dead against it; she thought it was a sign of decadence. She knew that boys were cheaper to procure and maintain but their useful life in our profession is very short as compared to girls. And then, you also have to see to it that the girls do not have anything to do with these boys. I thought she had a point there." Gulbadan told her friend.

"At times life is so difficult, isn't it?" Salamat sighed. "But one has to move on."

Farzana

As days passed, Jaddan grew very close to Gulbadan. She spent long hours chatting with her. Salamat had interrupted the story of Nur Bai's life. They resumed their conversation once Salamat bid goodbye.

"Once Nur Bai fell ill." Gulbadan began. " I was by her bed all the time but she insisted that I should relax and that the maid would look after her. After her recovery she called me to her room and told me, that after her I would head the *haveli*. I would inherit it with all other assets. She had already drawn up a will and had it recorded with the Nazim of Delhi. I had no words to thank her for this magnanimity. She replied that I was the only person who was really close to her heart. That's how I inherited this haveli. It has been inextricably linked with my life.'

"But tell me, Jaddo," Gulbadan asked Jaddan. 'When I met you on the steps of Jama Masjid you said that this *haveli* was the only place where you spent a few happy years of your life. Did you really mean it? I had thought you were upset with me for sending you away.'

"No, *chaudharayan*! This haveli was indeed a source of joy for me. You might remember that I was the daughter of a *Kanchani*, I don't know who my father was. My mother had once told me, that she used to work for a petty *kotha* patronized by casual labourers with very modest incomes. Sometimes *palki* bearers would come in droves to the *kotha* after they had carried some well known dancers to the house of a rich businessman or a noble for a *mujra*, and were let off for a couple of hours. She had come to this haveli and left me here when I was still a child. She herself was leading a life of misery and she wanted me to move up in life, and lead a life of honour and comfort. You were kind enough to give me shelter. You tried to train me in kathak, vocal and instrumental music. I could not meet the expectations of your sophisticated patrons, and after a few years you sent me with a drunken old Sayyad, a farmer of Baghpat.

His first begum made my life a hell. He died a few years later. His son from the first wife started harassing me. I could not stand it any longer, and one day, early in the morning I slipped out of the house with my daughter. Luckily, I came across a bullock cart carrying bags of wheat going to Delhi. I paid the owner five *paise*, and he allowed us to sit on the wheat bags. That was how we reached Shah Jahan Abad. *Chaudhrayan,* your *haveli* is the only home I have known in my unfortunate life."

Days passed by. Suddenly one day Jaddan fell seriously ill.

Despite Gulbadan's best efforts, she did not survive. For a while, Farzana was inconsolable, but soon she reconciled with her mother's death.

Farzana had grown into a beautiful woman though she was of short built. She was clever and cunning, and had a mind of her own. She soon realised that she was the leading light of Gulbadan's kotha. Once when Gulbadan was invited for a *mujra* in the Red Fort in honour of some guests, Farzana accompanied her. Farzana too danced and she drew much appreciation. She was overwhelmed with the grandeur of Diwan Khas and wondered if she could visit the hallowed precincts of the Fort again.

Farzana soon found it difficult to suppress her growing physical urges. Once when Gulbadan was away, she seduced an errand boy who used to bring supplies of *pan* and other accessories to the *haveli*. She derived so much pleasure from her first experience that she was always looking for an opportunity to make love to the hapless boy. Gulbadan got the wind of the goings on, but she ignored the matter. Later, it was known that Farzana was pregnant and in due time, a baby girl was born to her. Much to her surprise, every body including Gulbadan congratulated her. Sweets were distributed. One of the eunuchs called Marzai, said to Farzana:

"You are very lucky that you had a girl. She will grow up to be a *tawaif* and bring wealth to this house. If it were a boy, he would have been worthless and we would have had to support him."

Farzana often used to wonder how Marzai had landed in the *haveli*; this was an opportune moment.

"Marzai, tell me, how did you happen to come here?"

'Long story, Farzo! I am an Arab by birth. When I was a small boy some Portuguese sailors abducted me from my small coastal village in Arabia. They brought me to Goa in their *dhow* and castrated me there. Then they sold me to a slave trader who brought me to Delhi. He tried to sell me to various establishments. Nur Bai offered him the price he demanded."

"It must have been very hard on you!"

"Yes. If only I had been a girl my abductors would have sold me to a kotha like this one where life would have been much more comfortable."

"Shall I ask you something? Do you ever feel like making love to a girl?"

"I was attracted to a girl in this very *haveli*. I once kissed her and pressed her breasts. She only laughed and said, 'poor chap!'"

Responsibilities of motherhood sobered Farzana. She was genuinely fond of her child. After a few days of rest Farzana resumed dancing in the *mehfil*.

Farzana was still much sought after.

Walter

One winter evening, a tall, rugged, robust man with a mild stoop came to the *haveli*. He was very fair with a shock of silver-grey leonine hair. Farzana's beauty charmed the man, and he turned up at the *haveli* very often. Farzana too was fascinated by his rugged appearance and unusual hair. Slowly, Gulbadan became conscious of the visitor's infatuation with Farzana.

After a few days, Gulbadan decided to talk to Farzana on the matter. She called Farzana to her room and said:

"Farzo, I am getting old. Nowadays I feel very tired. I want to shut down my business. I had promised your mother that I would always look after your interests. I am afraid, the prospects, even for you, here, are not good. I understand that the new Nawab of Awadh has moved his court from Faizabad to Lucknow. Like his late father, he too is a great admirer of beautiful women. If you can move to Lucknow, your future will be assured. But if you do not want to go to Lucknow, there is another option." Gulbadan paused for a second.

Farzana looked at her, anxious. What was she going to suggest?

"There is this tall fair man from Europe. He works for the Jat Rajah, and is based at Agra." Suddenly, Farzana looked down. Her heart beat faster.

"He has a body of troops who call him, their General. This gentleman claims to be very close to the Jat Rajah and advises him on issues of war with other Rajahs of Rajputana and the chiefs in the neighbourhood. He takes part in various campaigns undertaken by the Rajah. He told me that he was keen to marry you. Well, I told him that you are my daughter. Then he said that he would treat you like a princess and that he could afford a luxurious and comfortable life as he had acquired a good fortune through his military campaigns.

But yes, he must be many years older than you. He has a wife too, who is said to be ill. She stays in Delhi with their son. And the General lives in Agra, which is not far from here." Gulbadan could see that Farzana was getting nervous.

"I told him that he has to ensure your future security, in case you agree to become his wife. He has given me his word that he would make a will, which would make you the heir to all his assets. This is the time to to decide on your future. If you decide to marry him, your child will stay on in the *haveli;* she will be looked after till you want her to stay with you. But whatever you decide I advise you not to tell anyone about the child; in the *kothas* a girl child is always welcome irrespective

of her paternity, but in the normal society it can become a handicap."

Farzana could not reach a conclusion suddenly. She wanted to weigh the pros and cons of the situation and asked for some time to ponder over the options. Gulbadan agreed but cautioned her that the General wanted to leave for Agra in a day or two, and he would like her to go with him.

Farzana thought over the matter, and realised that becoming the second wife of the General offered her an opportunity to advance in life. Life in a *kotha* would be uncertain especially when her dancing skills were nothing much to brag about. And then, the effective life of a dancer of a *kotha* was rather short; an ambitious woman would have to start her own establishment and become a *chaudhrayan*. The prospects of such establishments were rather bleak going by the experiences of Gulbadan and Salamat Jaan. The General was rather old, but life with him would be more dignified and broadly independent. Farzana was a shrewd woman. Before taking a decision, she even considered her prospects if she survived the General.

Gulbadan was happy to know about Farzana's decision. Before she set out on her journey to Agra, Gulbadan hugged her and gave her a pair of gold bracelets as a parting gift. Her eyes were moist and her heart heavy.

"Farzo dear, you are just a child. You have to learn the ways of the world. Never tell your husband that you are not a virgin;

he will love you all the more. On your first night, keep a pin or a needle and without him knowing it, draw a little blood from your thigh and let a drop spill on to the bed sheet. I hope you understood what I said."

The next evening, the General brought a covered bullock driven cart with curtains on both sides for Farzana. The General sauntered along on a horse. They were followed by armed guards and two torch-bearers. Farzana was troubled deep within. She had set out on a journey with a complete stranger, what did the future had in store for her? Lost in turbulent thoughts, she fell asleep. When she woke up early in the morning, she could make out that the sun had still not risen. As she parted the curtains aside to look outside, she heard the General's voice in broken Urdu:

"Darling, how are you? We are near Braj. We will spend the day with a friend of mine and shall leave in the evening."

She did not know how she should address the General. She said:

"Sir, I had a very sound sleep. But you must be very tired as you have travelled the whole night on horse back."

The General was amused.

"My name is Walter Sombre. You can call me Walter. I shall call you Begum. Ah yes, rididng a horse is no big deal for me, Begum. Do not forget that I am a seasoned soldier. I can travel by horse for much longer distances without any discomfort."

The next morning, they arrived at the rather modest

residence of Sombre, located within the Agra fort. It was furnished in European style. Farzana was dumbfounded by the grandeur of it, and thought it was even more majestic than the Red Fort of Delhi.

Sombre called a Kazi and formally married Farzana according to Muslim rites. He told her that he already had another wife and a son, Zafaryab, about eight years old. He was happy to learn that she had known about this fact before, and had still agreed to live with him.

As he had promised Gulbadan, Sombre drew up a will making Farzana the only beneficiary of his assets. He also explained to her that she would be quite secure within the Fort, even when he was away on duty. The Fort was under the control of the Jat Rajah. Sombre was in charge of its safety and security.

As Sombre took her around the fort, he told her about his humble origins in Austria in Europe. He was a carpenter on a French man-of-war and had travelled from Europe to South India, and then to Bengal. There he joined as a soldier in the army of the Nawab. He was promoted to the position of a sergeant within a short time. After a short while, he received the command of a battalion by the Nawab of Bengal in his army. But Sombre was not happy with his life in Bengal. He had raised the battalion himself so he moved westwards with his corps. He offered his services to different Nawabs and Rajahs in the heart of Hindustan and received handsome rewards. He was offered by the Jat Rajah regular service, and his corps was put up in Agra. His job required him to frequently go on military campaigns.

Sombre found that his bride had a genuine interest in what he was saying.

"Mughal Emperor's vizier Nujjuf Khan is very keen to wrest control of Agra Fort from the Jat Rajah and is always on the look out for opportunities. But then, there is nothing to worry as of now."

Farzana was quite excited with the ambience and aura of the Agra Fort. She was thrilled to see the mausoleum of Mumtaz Mahal built by Emperor Shahjahan on the banks of the river Yamuna, not far from the fort. She had heard a lot about this building but it was the first time she set her eyes on it.

On the first evening, Walter and Farzana sat down for dinner together. It was a good spread – roast mutton, roast chicken, beef-steak among other things.

Before dinner, Walter poured out a large whisky for himself.

"Have you ever tried whisky?"

"We were not allowed any liqour by the *Chaudhrayan*".

"O.K, then. We start you on claret."

He poured out a small quantity of the wine and offered it to Farzana. She had a sip and liked it. Walter poured a little more wine for her and helped himself to another tot of whisky. As they ate their food and enjoyed their drink, Walter said to Farzana.

"You are very young, Begum. I wonder if you have had any experience of sex?"

"Oh! No." Farzana remembered Gulbadan's advice.

"Well then, you may find the first experience a little painful. I will be careful not to hurt you too much."

Having charged himself with drinks, he asked Farzana if she would like more wine. She declined saying it had already gone to her head.

"Good. Now you take off your clothes, let me see you in all your glory."

Farzana hesitated. Walter laughed:

"Come on, this is going to be a daily affair."

Walter looked on while she undressed.

"Marvellous! God has been very kind to you when he created you."

He was absolutely bewitched by her silky smooth skin and alabaster like complexion.

Bouts of lovemaking continued for a few days. And when they were somewhat satiated one evening, over the drinks, Farzana asked:

"How do I compare with Barri Bibi?"

"I had picked her up from a modest *kotha* many years back. She has given me a son but she has always been a passive player in bed. Sex with her was like masturbating. But you are an absolute delight. Now I don't have to bother her. And I want to have a son by you.'

"Allah willing, your wish would be fulfilled."

After a little pause, Farzana said.

"But Walter, you must have had many other women."

"Darling, I am 45. I have had my flings but now that you are with me, I am sure there will be no necessity to sow wild oats anymore."

"But tell me, what was your most interesting experience with a woman?"

Walter pondered over for a moment and said:

"This happened long ago, just two years after I had come to India. I was based in Calcutta. I had no money and no standing. I had taken up a job as an ordinary soldier and was very lonely and quite frustrated. I used to visit a *kotha*. I am not sure whether I should tell all this, you may feel disturbed."

Farzana protested:

"Not at all, Walter. I know that all men are polygamous animals. Look at the Nawabs and Rajahs, they have numerous women at their command. As long as you are pleased with me, why should I get jealous of anybody who you had met many years ago."

"OK, if you are sure, I will tell you the whole story. One day at the kotha I saw a copper coloured, buxom young woman of medium height. I could not speak English or Bengali. Till then I could only speak French. As I was about to leave, she

30

came near me and said in her broken English:

'I come.'

She held me by the arm and gestured with her hands and made me move. I brought her to my small apartment. I had no servant then, and I used to cook for myself. She followed me to the kitchen. I understood from her gestures that she wanted to cook for both of us. As she was cooking, I helped myself to some whisky. I went to the kitchen and asked her through gestures if she would like some whisky. She smiled and shook her head. After we had had our food, we went to the bedroom. She took off her clothes. She had a terrific sexy figure, though she was not beautiful. She had immense breasts. But she was quite smelly. I was aroused and taking off my clothes I took her in my arms and started sucking her breasts and then kissed her on the lips. She held my member and dragged me to the bed. She said, 'Me, a tribal. Give baby.'

I hesitated. I did not want to get involved in any complication. I put on the sheath, but she pulled it off. And lying in bed, she guided my member into her and pressed my whole body with her hands, forcefully, as if she was not sure whether I would go through with it. When it was over, she smiled and caressed me repeatedly."

"It is a very interesting tale. I remember, *Chaudhrayan* once said that a tribal girl wanted to have a child before marriage, they believe that it improved her marriage prospects. And I suppose if the child is fathered by an European, her chances brighten up further.'

"The tale is not over as yet. That tribal girl did not leave my apartment. I was bubbling with energy; she too was youthful. She made me have sex with her in different poses, sometimes, all through the day. When I did not respond to some of her ideas, she said, 'See temples.'

I didn't have a clue as to what she was saying. After about a month she said, pointing to her tummy, 'Baby here. I go.'

I tried to offer her some money but she would not take any, pointing all the time to her stomach. I did not know her name, and she did not know mine. She did not try to contact me ever, even though I was in Calcutta for quite some time. The child, boy or girl, should be grown up by now."

"Have you ever missed her?"

"Sometimes I did, but now that you are with me, what more do I want!"

Once their honeymoon days were over, Sombre decided to train his wife for future responsibilities. He wanted her to learn horse riding.

"Horse is a noble and useful animal. It is far superior to bullocks, which are so much in use in Hindustan. In times of war, horses ridden by determined soldiers can create havoc in the enemy ranks."

Sombre introduced Farzana to the officers of his corps. There were over 200 of them, mostly Europeans.

"Eventually you may have to command this corps, after I am gone." Walter told her.

Farzana protested saying, "Please, Walter. I pray to Allah to give you a long life."

Deep in her heart, Farzana was quite excited about the prospect of ultimately heading the troop; never ever in her wildest dreams had she fancied this possibility. Under Walter's guidance she started socialising with the officers and soldiers. She would go round the military lines, on horseback. She was in charge of their welfare, and found time to personally supervise their wellbeing. If someone fell ill, she would spend hours with the sick trooper or officer.

Not surprisingly, she became very popular with the entire Sombre's corps.

Decaying Delhi

After a few years of his marriage with Farzana, Walter's first wife, Barri-Bibi fell seriously ill. He had to visit Delhi to ensure proper treatment for her and to sort out some family matters. Farzana obtained permission to stay with Gulbadan Jaan while they were in Delhi.

As she entered the *haveli* she was surprised to see a wall between the lowest terrace and the rest of the complex, right across the courtyard with only a door in the corridor. Gulbadan came out of her room and Farzana cried out:

"*Chaudhrayan!* Why, have you constructed the wall?"

"I am no longer *a Chaudhrayan.* I will call your child, Nooro, but don't let her know that you are her mother. Tell her that you are her *Khala*. She has grown into a pretty and sweet child and lightens the burden of my misfortunes with her prattle. I am very grateful to you for leaving your child with me.'

"But before you call her, tell me about the wall. I am so impatient to know."

"When I shut down the *kotha,* I found the empty building so huge that it started giving me the feeling of a haunted house. I started getting nightmares. Often in dreams, I would see visions of Nur Bai coming out of her bedroom in dancing clothes, and gliding daintily on the top terrace of the courtyard right across the *haveli.* Sometimes I would get up screaming. Then Salamat Bai advised me to build this wall. Now I can sleep peacefully."

When Farzana saw Nooro she was beside herself with joy and sorrow. She hugged the child tightly and kissed her. Nooro was bewildered. Farzana gave her a basket of *laddoos.*

In the evening, after dinner, Farzana sat down to talk to Gulbadan.

"Tell me all about yourself, Farzo. How does the *firang*i treat you? Are you happy?" Gulbadan was anxious to know.

"Walter is very kind and considerate to me. I am fortunate to have married him."

"You can't imagine how glad and relieved I am to hear this from you. When I sent you with him, I was quite worried. He is so much older to you. Does that worry you?"

"After a miserable past, what better future could I have hoped for? *Chaudhrayan*, how is life treating you?"

"Life in Delhi, for every body, has become much worse than it was when you were here. Now, please stop calling me *Chaudhrayan*, Farzo; if you don't mind call me Amma."

"But Amma, you have a house to live in and you have your

savings too; what's worrying you then?"

"I can say I am financially okay, at least for the time being. I even have a whole time maid who takes care of Nooro and me. I was essentially talking about people who have no regular income of their own. The law and order has totally broken down and no decent person feels safe in this city. Robbers and dacoits indulge in their nefarious activities with impunity. Faulad Khan, the Kotwal of Delhi is said to be involved in these crimes. Mind you, this is a secret. The other day one of his agents came to meet me and complained that I had not sent the monthly protection money for many months. When I told him that I had shut down my business and that I had no income, he would not believe me. He went round the *haveli* and also made enquiries in the neighbourhood. Lies and deceit reign supreme here. As the poet said:

> *Ai jhoot, aaj shahr mein tera hi daur hai,*
> *Shewa yehi sabhon ka, yehi sab ka taur hai.*

O lie, you are the lord supreme of this city estate,
You are the creed of people's life, you are the popular faith.

> *Ai jhoot tu shiaar hua sari khalak ka,*
> *Kya shah ka, kya wazir ka, kya ahl-e-daliq ka*

Every one accepts your writ, adores you day and night.
Be he a king, or vice- regent, or a humble man.
"You are indeed marvellous. You can remember the ghazals.

Who wrote these lines?"

"Mir Taqi Mir. I spend lot of my idle hours reading and reciting compositions of the famous Urdu poets. They provide me good company. Talking of lies, I must also tell you a current story doing the rounds in Delhi these days. It says an employee of a prominent minister of Shah Alam, who often took liberties with his boss, once came to see the minister and was asked,

What news?

Not much, only a merchant has arrived with four cart-loads of lies for the use of Your Honour.

Is that all? Why, I can eat up all of it in a day!"

Farzana smiled, and suddenly her mind became lighter. After all, she had made the right decision at the right point of time.

Warrior

"I would like to go with you on a military campaign."

Walter was surprised at his Begum's words. He guffawed.

"My lady, fighting is a serious business. Do you know how dangerous it is?"

"I can guess Walter. Still I would like to have first hand experience of an actual battle." Farzana knew what she was demanding.

"That is very courageous of you! Indeed, if you are that keen we may get an opportunity in the near future. But before that it will be desirable to understand the organizational structure of my corps. You must grasp the role of the *subedar* and the *jemadar* in day-to-day life of the troops and when a battle is on. Our soldiers are all simpletons. They come from very poor backgrounds. Their income is meagre; they risk their lives for about four rupees per month. But they are very devoted to their commanders and will obey any orders, if they have faith in them. I consider them as my own kith and kin. As far as possible, I never expose them to unnecessary risk. I withdraw my troops if I find that there is no chance of victory."

"I thought everybody who takes to the profession of arms has essentially pecuniary motivation." Farzana wanted to know.

"That is true in a way. We come from distant lands, yet we take to soldiering here, mainly for making fortunes. No wonder, then, we are called mercenaries. Of course, many become soldiers with a sense of adventure."

"Why are there so many whites and half-castes in senior positions in your corps?"

"I don't want to denigrate the locals, but Europeans make better officers and leaders. The Indian soldiers prefer to serve under white officers, they have more faith in their sense of fair play and justice. From the Commander's point of view, I can tell you I have more faith in their capacity to ensure discipline in the force. An indisciplined force is totally ineffective. When it comes to ensuring discipline, you must be ruthless."

"Do you offer *namaz* before going into battle?" Farzana asked rather innocently.

Walter laughed.

"I thought you knew that I am a Christian. But no, I don't go to church and don't even offer routine prayers. You can call me a non-practicing Christian."

Farzana was eager to know more. "Who are Christians? Can you tell me more about them?"

Walter was surprised at her enthusiasm. He said.

"Less than eighteen hundred years ago a messenger of God called Christ appeared in Bethlehem. He was a man of compassion and peace and talked against injustice. His followers compiled his message in a book called The Bible. His followers are called Christians. Their places of worship are called churches. There is one in Agra too. Emperor Akbar had gifted this land."

"You should take me to this church with you."

The Jat Rajah had already appointed Walter the Administrator of Agra. The small Christian community at Agra was delighted. The church building was still unfinished and though Father Wendell tried his best he could not go forward with his mission due to financial constraints. Appointment of Walter came as a God sent opportunity. Father Wendell invited Walter and his Begum to visit the church under renovation. As he expected, Sombre extended financial help from his personal resources to complete the construction.

When the church was finally built, the Administrator was invited to inaugurate the completed church. Farzana found the serene atmosphere in the church, and the brotherhood of the congregation quite unique. Subsequently, she wondered whether it were the Christian virtues which were responsible for the success of the British Arms in Hindustan.

It was after sometime that Nujjuf Khan, the vizier of the Moghul Emperor Shah Alum decided to get back the Agra Fort from the Jat Rajah, and moved his forces to wrest control from the Bharatpur Kingdom. The Jat Rajah tried to defend his possessions with the help of Walter Sombre. On the insistence of Farzana, Walter allowed her to join the expedition, warning her all the time that it could be very risky. To the surprise of the entire Walter's corps, she rode a horse with the raised sword in her hand and charged the enemies like other soldiers. A select band of Walter's troopers provided protection to her, but a musket shot whizzed past her left ear. The Begum was frightened out of her wits. She saw the carnage and heard the shrieks of the wounded and the dying. The Moghuls won the battle. The Jat Rajah and Walter just manged to escape capture.

Her first experience of war made Farzana wiser.

"Fighting is a terrible and inhuman affair. I would not have understood the reality of war, if I had not seen it from close quarters. Why do we have to fight at all?"

"It might be true Begum. But don't forget that since the world began, fighting has been a part of human survival. Those who are not prepared to fight, suffer severe setbacks. Haven't you heard of Nadir Shah, the Iranian who killed thousands of people in Delhi, carrying away women, leaving their relatives in utter despire? He carried the whole wealth of Delhi leaving the Emperor virtually a pauper. Those who are not prepared for war are doomed to be destroyed; that is what history teaches us." Sombre offered.

Moghul vizier was overwhelmed by the gallantry and

discipline of Walter's corps even in adversity. After the hostilities were over, he offered liberal terms and handsome rewards to Walter to join him with his corps, which was accepted.

Farzana's stratagem to ride into battle, on horseback with a raised sword in hand became the talk of the whole of Hindustan. The Jats, the Maratha and the Moghuls, were all captivated by the tales of the beautiful warrior. The story as it passed on from one mouth to another kept on acquiring brighter colours. In no time Farzana turned a heroine, and the queen of Walter's corps.

Empress

Mahadhji Scindia, the Maratha Chief, an ally of the Moghul King, was talking to Rane Khan, his friend and a General of his army.

"She is a crafty courtesan; without shedding a drop of blood and not as much as a scratch on her body, she has become a heroine."

"If, I, an illiterate water carrier can become your General, why can't a courtesan be a warrior?" Rane Khan argued.

"Indeed! Well said! Mark my words, she will go far in life. I would like to have her on my side."

"They say, her beauty is enhanced by a sound mind. She has a very good sense of judgement and a practical approach to political problems. If so, she can be trusted to help her husband who is always seeking to go over to the winning side, to spot a winner. There is every chance that your wish be fulfilled. But I shall urge you not to fall for her charms."

Mahadhji smiled,

"Well, you can never be sure!"

The Agra Fort reverted to the Moghul control after their victory over the Jat Rajah. Even though Sombre's corps had not been successful in the campaign, their reputation as a disciplined force soared high. After Walter joined Nujjaf Khan, the Emperor invited Walter to meet him in his palace in the Red Fort. He went there, dressed as a Moghul nobleman and presented his salaams and *nazrana* in the traditional Moghul style. The Emperor was pleased.

"We have heard of your military skill and the valour and discipline of your troops. We are confident, now that you have become our ally, your resources will be available for defending the Moghul Empire."

"Your Majesty! I am always at your command."

Soon after his audience with the Emperor, Sombre requested Nujjaf Khan, the all-powerful vizier, for a *jagir* so that he could maintain his corps with the income. He also petitioned the Emperor for a *jagir*. Walter was busy in various military campaigns and Farzana had to pursue the request. With Walter's permission, she called on the Begum of the vizier.

As vizier's Begum set eyes on Farzana she exclaimed:

"MashaAllah! What a pretty face! God has been kind to you, but tell me how can such a delicate person take to fighting? We hear that you fought against our troops."

"It was my folly. I beg your forgiveness."

"Now that your husband has become our ally, all is forgotten."

Farzana spent about two hours with the Begum talking on the affairs of Hindustan and about the English who were then, throwing their weight about. As Farzana rose to leave, the Begum said:

"You are welcome to our house for any assistance that you may need."

Farzana was quite happy with the reception she got from Vizier's Begum.

It was not long after this meeting that Walter returned from a military expedition to the North, where some aggressors had occupied a large tract of land to the east of river Yamuna. Walter was successful in defeating the rebels and restoring the territory to the Moghul Emperor. Walter went to the haveli of the vizier one evening to discuss something urgent and Farzana accompanied him to spend some time with the Begum. Farzana explained to the Begum the urgent need for a *jagir* to properly maintain the corps. She requested the Begum to intercede on their behalf for a *jagir* in the area, recently restored by Walter to the Emperor. She also expressed her wish to meet the Empress on an opportune occasion.

Id festival, an important occasion for the Muslims of the world, was round the corner. Begum felt that it would not look odd if Farzana accompanied her when she went to the palace to say '*Id-Mubarak*' to the Empress; it was the traditional greeting. Farzana carried a couple of exquisite strings of pearls to gift the Empress. She had taken along a gold bracelet for the Dowager Queen. As they were escorted to the *zenana,* next to Diwan-Khas pavillion, Begum of the Vizier said *adab* thrice to the Empress and offered the *nazrana.* Farzana, bringing to bear all her training by Gulbadan, made the triple *tasleem* to the Empress. Farzana offered the *nazrana* and wished her *Id-Mubarak.* Both of them said *adab* to the Dowager-Empress and made their offerings. The two ladies were invited to sit on the silk carpet in front of the Empress.

The Empress said to Farzana.

"I hear you are turning out to be a modern day Razia Sultana. We are living in very interesting times when pretty girls want to be warriors."

"Madam I am your slave, I shall do whatever you command."

The Empress was pleased. The first impression had made a lasting mark.

Jagirdar

Ultimately, the efforts of Walter and Farzana bore fruit and the Emperor granted him a *jagir* to the East of the river Yamuna near Meerut. The place was called Sardhana. Before shifting to the new place, Farzana wished to meet her daughter and Gulbadan. But she was now the Begum of a wellknown *jagirdar,* it was not proper to visit Gulbadan at her haveli; so she sent her a message to come over with Nooro.

The moment she saw her child, Farzana ran up to her and hugged her. She couldn't control her tears. Deep within she was burdened with a sense of guilt for not openly owning up her daughter. She had been debating in her mind whether to ignore the advise of Gulbadan – to keep the existence of her child a secret, or reveal everything to her husband. But she was sure that her future would be seriously jeopardized if Walter came to know that she had borne a child before marriage. So she ignord her heart's feelings and decided on what her head told her.

Gulbadan was ecstatic to see Farzo.

"You can't imagine how happy I am! Your husband has become an important member of the Mughal nobility. I am reminded of the day when I met you at the steps of Jama Masjid long ago. Your mother would have been so happy at your achievement in life."

"Now you are my Amma and Nooro's grandmother. But I must confess that I am bitterly torn in my heart for reasons that you can understand."

"I know your dilemma, Farzo. But, I feel that you should keep your secret for some more time."

As Gulbadan and Nooro were about to leave, Farzana gave Gulbadan quite a huge sum. Gulbadan protested, but Farzana said:

"Please keep it, Amma. It will help to lighten my mind's burden. From now on, I will send you money, regularly. Accept this, for my sake."

Soon, Walter was appointed Governor of Agra. He was given the responsibility of its civil administration and defense of the *subha*. Before going to Agra, they visited the lands of their *jagir*. They went around Sardhana and were pleasantly surprised to see that the tract was fertile, with plenty of water. The growing crops wore a healthy look.

They decided to live in an old Maratha fort till they constructed a new house at Sardhana.

Agra

In Agra, Walter and his begum stayed at their same old house where they used to live when he was with the Jat Rajah. The Christian community was very happy to have Walter Sombre and Farzana back at Agra. They hosted a reception in their honour, and the priest recalled Sombre's help, when construction of the Church was held up for want of funds. The community leaders requested Farzana to visit their homes even if Sombre could not find time.

The first house she went to was that of a so-called half-caste Christian; he was the son of a white trooper from a Jat girl. He had married a Rajput girl and had two children. When Farzana called on them, the younger child was down with high fever. Farzana, without caring for the protocol sat with the child on her cot and collected her in her arms. For a brief moment, she thought it was her Nooro. She had never been there for her daughter to give her enough love and care. How was she looked after when she fell ill? As she recovered from her reverie, she assured the parents that the best doctor in town would attend to their child. The parents were surprised and relieved to find that the Governor's wife was taking personal interest in their child.

Farzana told the Church leaders that she would look after their welfare and she should be informed if anyone fell sick. The Christian community of Agra was indebted to her, and Walter and Farzana turned an integral part of all their celebrations and gatherings.

Agra was the place in Hindustan where Sombre had stayed the longest. He felt very close to the Christians of Agra as they showered him with affection and regard. Now Sombre felt emotionally bonded to the place. He knew that he was nearing the eve of his life. He decided to build a house in Agra where Farzana could live on after he was gone. Once he was dead, the Emperor might not allow her to hold the jagir.

He acquired some land not far from Agra and started developing it as a garden. Walter took earnest interest in designing the house and supervising the construction.

Then one day, Walter fell ill. As his condition got worse, Walter asked the doctor to leave him for a short while; he wanted to talk to his Begum in confidence. When the two were by themselves, Walter said:

"Begum, I want to tell you something. You might be aware of it, atleast you must have heard some rumours."

The Begum drew closer.

"What I am telling you has weighed heavily on my conscience since very long. About thirty-two years ago, when I arrived from Europe to seek fortune in this country I got an opportunity to serve under Meer Cossim, the Nawab of Bengal. He had been suffering military reverses at the hands of the English. He gave me the command of a battalion of sepoys. He asked me to ensure strict discipline among his troops and promised to place more battalions under my command. I didn't want this opportunity to slip through my fingers. I had been doing odd petty jobs before; this was my chance to make it big. I wanted to please the Nawab in every possible way."

Walter's throat went dry. He took a sip of water.

"I am sure you will think very poorly of me, when you have heard the whole story but I have to tell you this. It is in your interest when I am no longer there."

"Don't bring such thoughts to your mind. I am sure you will recover within no time."

"Mir Cossim had his treasure and vital stores at Monghir. The English captured his treasure and the stores there. The Nawab was so incensed at this misfortune. Earlier, he had managed to take some English civilians and troops as prisoners. He was holding them in Patna; he ordered me to slaughter them all. I was in a queer dilemma – if I refused I could lose my command, if not my life. The Nawab was raving like a mad man screaming for revenge. I carried out his orders. I was merely obeying my employer, but since then the English have been after me."

Gasping, he went on.

"They have been pursuing me all over Hindustan. Wherever I went for contracts, whether in Awadh, Jaipur or even with the Emperor, they intimidated all of them. Only Nujjuf Khan ignored their threats. I am worried now that when I am gone they would try to take revenge on you. Do take care."

Walter's voice grew weak.

"I want to tell you, Begum, that I am leaving immense wealth for you. I acquired almost the whole of it when Mir Cassim refused to pay me and I plundered him. I did the same with the Nawab vizier of Awadh when he failed to pay my dues. I lived very frugally and so almost the entire wealth is at your command. Keep this information a secret and guard this wealth carefully."

Walter died in 1778 A.D. and Farzana was left alone to face the battles of her life.

The Corps

The first priority on Farzana's mind was to gain control over Samru's corps. She set about the task by cashing in on the sympathy of the officers of the corps who came to offer their condolences. She was certainly popular among the officers and the men. But Zafaryab, son of Sombre from his first Begum, laid his claim on the corps. He was known to be a dimwit among the corps, still he managed to get supporters.

Some senior European officers got together and discussed the issue of the leadership. They reached the conclusion that Zafaryab was not fit to lead the corps. They were not sure of his financial status either. Besides, all had come to know that Sombre or Samru, as he was popularly known, had bequeathed almost all his wealth to the Begum. It was therefore widely felt that only the Begum could assure regular income to the corps.

Threee senior European officers sought an interview with Nujjaf Khan, the vizier of the Emperor and explained their view.

"We have come to seek your support in the matter. The corps is essentially meant for providing support to your military operations. We are therefore keen that the corps should not suffer in its military capabilities after Walter's departure. But the Begum, being a woman, could face some difficulty in leading it."

Nujjaf Khan sat back and thought about it. "Frankly speaking, I think the Begum is quite capable of leading the corps, provided you gentlemen extend your full support and scotch any intrigues that are inevitable. In any case, I have to speak to the Emperor before I give my decision. Succession in this case also involves many administrative and political issues, you have talked only of the military side of it."

The officers of the corps were glad to learn that the vizier had no doubt about the Begum's abilities but they were not sure what the Emperor's reaction would be. They were seriously concerned about their own future as they were convinced that the corps would disintegrate, if Zafaryab were to be successful in his efforts.

At last, the vizier conveyed the Emperor's approval on the matter. Begum assumed command of the corps, in the presence of a few important nobles and officials of the Empire at a formal ceremony held in her late husband's land at Agra. The Christian leaders also took part in the ceremony of succession. The troops marched past their new commander, saluting her as she stood on a raised platform. Guns were fired in her honour. Begum gave a short speech assuring the troops that their welfare would be her primary concern.

Zafaryab was not invited and stayed sulking at Delhi.

The next urgent problem, facing Begum was to obtain an early title to the Sardhana *jagir*. Sardhana was central to her vision of the future of the corps as well as hers. Without Sardhana she would have no security and she would have to look up to the Emperor to maintain the corps. She didn't have much faith in the Emperor's capacity to pay for any military operations that might be undertaken on his behalf.

The Begum set about pursuing her objective with determination. She called on the vizier in her capacity as the commander of Walter's corps and explained her position. Fortunately for her, the Emperor had himself raised the issue of the *jagir* when the vizier had talked to him about the matter of succession to the corps. He had felt that the corps and the *jagir* could not be separated though he had agreed with the vizier that it was not essential that Sardhana should be passed onto Begum Samru and that she could be given some other *jagir* in lieu of her old one. The vizier was under intense pressure to give Sardhana to somebody else as it was rated to be one of the best tracts of land in the region.

Begum Samru had set her heart on Sardhana; she pleaded forcefully with the vizier. She also called on the vizier's Begum.

"I have to congratulate you on taking over Samru's corps. I wish you all success."

"I would be successful only if I were allowed to continue in Sardhana."

"I thought that would be a natural corollary. Any way, I shall put in a word for you in the quarters concerned."

Begum of the vizier sought the help of the queen who felt that Begum Samru deserved to retain Sardhana.

At last Begum Samru received Shah Alam's *sanad*, which granted her ownership of the *jagir* of Sardhana for her lifetime with clear legal title. The Begum was keen to personally express her gratefulness to both the queen and the Emperor, so she sought an appointment with the queen.

"I am most grateful to you for granting the jagir of Sardhana to me."

"It is the Emperor who should be thanked." The queen replied.

"I shall ever be beholden to you if you could convey my request to his majesty to be allowed to see him."

"The king is in the *tasbeah khana*. I shall go over and enquire if he can see you now."

Samru Begum accompanied by the queen, then proceeded to the front of *tasbeah khana*, with her veil on, and made three obeisances to the Emperor. She then went up to the *musnud* on which his majesty sat, and presented a nazarana, on a white scarf. The king accepted the gift and gave it to prince Akbar Shah who had arrived there.

Samru Begum said:

"Your Majesty, I am most grateful to you for having granted the *jagir* to me."

"We are very sorry on the demise of your husband, Walter Reinhardt Sombre, and extend genuine sympathy and condolences to you. We hope you are aware of the fact that on the very unfortunate death of your husband, you have taken on heavy responsibilities on your shoulders."

"Yes, your Majesty."

"You are, we presume, aware that you are the only lady jagirdar in our entire kingdom."

"Yes your Majesty."

"You also undoubtedly know that you are the only lady commander of a substantial military force."

"Yes, your Majesty."

"You are expected to keep a check on the Sikhs in the North. You have also to tackle the Rohillas, who can be quite troublesome."

"I can assure your Majesty that we shall discharge all our responsibilities to your entire satisfaction."

The Emperor then got up to signify the end of the interview. It was Samru's first direct encounter with Shah Alum. She was overwhelmed by his royal personality. He was in his fifty-fifth year and looked extremely dignified. He was tall and had a commanding stature. Begum Samru developed an instant liking for the emperor.

To ensure an assured, regular income to meet the expenses of the corps, Begum Samru undertook a thorough study of the revenue system, which brought her returns from the lands. She wanted to increase her earnings from the land and soon realised that the local revenue official called *patwari* was the lynchpin of the scheme for success. She studied the cropping pattern and the system of irrigating the farms. She went round the villages and talked to the farmers and discussed their problems. In due course, efforts to increase her income from the *jagir* bore fruit. Begum Samru started exploring new avenues to add to her wealth.

Baptism

Begum used to periodically visit Agra to look at her estate and to meet her Christian friends. She invariably visited the church and occasionally attended service. The leaders of the Christian community observed that the Begum was almost a Christian in her outlook. Father Gregory suggested to her.

"I can see that you are genuinely interested in our community. I think you will feel more at home with us if you embrace our faith formally."

"To say you the truth, I am not a religious person. I grew up as a Muslim but was never a devoted one. I need a little time to think over this."

Begum Samru deliberated on what the priest said. She recalled her discussions with Walter. He had once said:

"In my search for a fortune in this land, I have had to deal with as many as fourteen native Nawabs and Rajahs and I observed that none of them has the capability to resist the Christian led forces of the Europeans. You are conversant with the state of affairs in Delhi, the Mughal capital. You will agree that the Mughal Empire is gasping for its last breath. I feel that Christians will rule this land in not too distant future."

Her life revolved around her corps. She felt that her European officers, who were all Christians, would be happy if she formally embraced the Christian faith. And, she had yet another motive as well. Begum Samru felt that her leverage with the East India Company, whose star was in the ascendant, would improve if she were to become a Christian. She was baptised as a Roman Catholic on the 7 May 1781.

After about a month of her conversion, an abnormally violent dust storm swept Delhi. Later there was a massive earthquake. A meteor had fallen near Jhajjar not far from Delhi. She learnt that Gulbadan's haveli developed some cracks. On her return from Agra, she went to meet Gulbadan and Nooro and to see the damage to the building. She was relieved to find out that the damage was not serious.

Nujjaf

Soon after, Begum Samru's benefactor Mirza Nujjaf Khan was elevated to the post of Regent of the Mughal empire. He was made the Commander-in-Chief and was given authority of all forces by Shah Alam. Begum Samru went over to meet Nujjaf's chief Begum, whom she was very friendly with.

"Allah has heard our prayers! The Empire is now safe from its enemies."

She gifted a valuable diamond-studded bracelet to Nujjaf's Begum.

"I thank you for your well wishes and the gorgeous present. I am sure the Regent will always watch your interests."

Nujjaf's administrative skills and astuteness in military operations brought order and harmony in the Empire. He was able to improve the economy of the government too. When Shah Alam decided to celebrate the marriage of his second and favourite son Prince Akbar Shah, Nujjaf offered to hold the ceremony at his house. The marriage was a splendid affair.

Begum Samru took the opportunity to present valuable gifts of diamond -studded bracelets to the bride and strings of purest possible pearls to Prince Akbar.

It was essential for any influential person within the Empire to be well informed about the goings on within the Mughal court and the Red Fort. Begum Samru had a team of informers who kept her posted with the latest developments in Delhi.

Fortunes of the empire were short lived. Nujjaf fell under the evil influence of Latafat Ali Khan, a eunuch, a general of the Awadh army who had wedded Mahtab, a loose woman of bewitching beauty. Latafat had been seconded to the Mughal army as he was close to Nujjaf. He introduced his wife to the Regent, who ensnared him, luring him with wine and women. An abstemious soldier, who had never tasted forbidden drinks or cast his eye on any woman of ill repute, was frolicking in private wine parties in the company of women of dubious character. It was in one such party that Nujjaf revealed one of his desires to Mahtab.

"I find Begum Samru extremely beautiful. It has been my ambition to spend a night with her. Can you persuade her to do this favour for me?"

"Why not? After all, she was a *kothawali*." Mahtab was confident.

Mahtab called on Begum Samru, as the wife of a General of the Mughal army. After a few pleasantries she said:

"You know the Regent is a great admirer of yours."

"He has been very kind to me. He has placed an additional battalion under my command, after he became the Regent. It is a great honour. I shall ever remain grateful to him."

"He will be even more helpful and kind to you if you mix with him socially. You are single, you should have no difficulty in accepting his invitation to attend a party."

"Will his chief Begum attend such a party?"

"Madame, do try to understand. How can the Regent mingle with other women if his Begum is around?"

Begum Samru saw through Mahatab's ploy. She did not want to use strong language, lest she should talk ill of her to the Regent. She excused herself citing her compulsions.

She was very upset at Mahtab's comments. She knew that her past must have encouraged Mahatab to consider her an easy game. Lying in bed, she cried in frustration; her thoughts turned towards her daughter Nooro and Gulbadan. She decided to invite Gulbadan to stay with her; and then she would be able to make up for the days she had to live away from her daughter.

Nujjaf Khan developed consumption. Coupled with a life of dissipation, he expired in April 1782 after a regency of about four years.

Sardhana

Gulbadan's eyes overflowed when she turned back to look at Nur Bai's haveli one last time. Nooro couldn't understand why her Amma was so heartbroken to leave behind the empty dilapidated haveli.

"Why are you so upset? I thought you were very pleased when we received the invitation from *Khala* to live with her."

"Nooro, my dear, I have stayed in this *haveli* for the last forty years. I have had a very hectic, colourful but yet comfortable life. I am reminded of the first time when I stepped into this place. I was about six years old then. I saw Nur Bai and thought she was some fairy queen. She had been very kind to me all through my life. The only one thing I could hold against her is that she did not allow me to marry and lead a life of my choice. Well, one can't get every thing in life."

Nooro, however, was very excited. On the eve of their departure for Sardhana, an old woman, who had been living in their neighbourhood for the last many years, had come over to see Nooro.

"I am really glad that at last Farzana has owned you up. She is your Amma. She left you with the *chaudhrayan,* when she married that *firanghee,*" she had said.

Nooro had often wondered why the Begum became very emotional whenever she set eyes on her. Now she knew the reason. But she decided not to ask anyone about it.

Begum Samru had sent a special bullock-cart with roof and curtains for the journey. A platoon of troops from Sardhana battalion based at Delhi was detailed for their protection. They started very early in the morning. They knew nothing much about Delhi, but just the town within the great wall around the city. Now, they crossed the river Yamuna by a bridge of boats. As they moved north there were wheat fields all over. They chose to rest for a night in a village called Jatana, where an officer of the Begum's corps received them.

Early next morning, they started out for Sardhana. They observed that the fields were greener, healthier. On the way, they stopped at a well to drink water. Nooro observed an interesting contraption at the well. A thick wooden pole was supported horizontally on two wooden posts, on either side across the well. The pole carried a pulley. A rope was wound round the revolving pulley, which was being pulled by a black bullock walking down the ramp, dug in the ground. As they waited at the well, a big leather bag emerged out of the well full of water, which was tilted by a helper, into a trough made of stone and mortar. Water was flowing from the trough into a small channel for irrigating the fields. As soon as the leather bag was emptied, it was lowered into the well and the bullock started walking up the ramp, made in a circular fashion. Both Nooro and Gulbadan found this concept very exciting.

A man clad in a loincloth and wearing a sacred thread, was bathing nearby. Nooro looked on intently at him and, Gulbadan's experienced eyes didn't miss to notice it. She realised that the girl had come of age.

"He is a handsome brahman youth." Gulbadan commented.

Nooro blushed.

The Begum was waiting for them impatiently. She received them warmly, hugging Gulbadan and kissing Nooro.

"I hope you had a good journey." She said.

"Yes, Farzo, a ver interesting journey, indeed. We saw this well on our way, and Nooro found the whole system of drawing water from the well very thrilling. She insisted on watching the leather bag coming up and going down. We spent more than an hour by the well.'

"We have lots of such wells. My *jagir* virtually lies between two streams, Yamuna and Hindon. So, our wells are never short of water. And we can irrigate our fields as and when there is need for water for the crops. Our peasantry is flourishing and our revenues too are rising. Now the other chiefs have become jealous of me."

Gulbadan felt proud of Farzana.

Gulbadan and Nooro were amazed by the life the Begum led. She had numerous maids, retainers and security guards. The luxurious carpets and European furniture dazzled them.

"I could never have imagined that you are doing so well, your late mother would have been so happy." Gulbadan said.

Nooro filled the Begum's life with happiness, and her heart with peace. Now, she never felt lonely.

Gulbadan continued to teach Urdu and Farsi to Nooro who, however, was not very keen on studies. Gulbadan taught her to play chess, which was a popular pastime with the gentry of that era. Nooro was more interested in meeting people and moving about around her Khala's residence. Many foreign and native officers of Sardhana's corps came to see the Begum to discuss various issues. A French officer, Darribere, was a frequent visitor. One day, he happened to see the young girl in her full bloom and was quite surprised.

"I have never seen you here earlier, who are you?"

"My name is Nooro."

She did not wish to reveal anything more.

"Well! Nooro, can we be friends? We can play games like marbles and chess."

"Certainly. I can help you to improve your Urdu and Farsi."

"That will be very nice." Darribere said. "Have you ever gone riding a horse? There are very good ponies here and the countryside is very pretty with thick forests."

"I am scared of horses."

Darribere laughed.

"I will teach you how to handle a pony. You will start loving horses then."

Darribere started visiting Samru's house more frequently. He persuaded Nooro to go riding with him. They explored the countryside together. They went on their ponies along the banks of Yamuna to watch boats drifting along. Together they observed travelers being ferried across the Yamuna and Hindon. Once they got down and started walking along the bank of Hindon, holding the reins of their ponies. They moved towards a thick grove, and tied the ponies to a tree. Darribere pulled Nooro towards him and kissed her passionately. Observing her shared pleasure, he dragged her down on to the ground and made love to her. Nooro was swept off her feet by the first experience of sex.

Darribere said,

"Let us get married. I have to go on a military operation shortly. On my return we can get formally married, of course, with the permission of the Begum Sahiba."

Gulbadan noticed the mutual attraction of Nooro and the Frenchman. She smiled to herself noticing that Nooro had the same fascination for Europeans, as her mother had.

Soon Darribere had to go out on duty. Nooro missed him badly and pined for him night and day. Gulbadan understood her misery and tried to keep her company.

Zebun-Nissa

There was practically no governance at the seat of the Mughal empire. The Regent, Nujjaf Khan, had been incapacitated by serious ailments and no decisions were taken. Soon Nujjuf died (1782 A.D.) of consumption. An era ended with his departure.

After Nujjaf's death, the scene at the court was again chaotic with various claimants seeking to be appointed Regent. Shah Alam, after some disastrous appointments, picked on Mahadhji Sindhia to the posts of the Regent as well as the supreme Commander-in-Chief of the Army of the Empire. Begum Samru felt that the latest incumbent would last for quite some time. She sought an audience from him through General Rane Khan who was known to be very close to Mahadhji.

When she met the new Regent Rane Khan was also with him.

The Regent said, "From now on, you will be responsible for the protection of the empire's northern borders west of river Yamuna, where we could have some trouble from our adversaries. Please ensure that your battalions are in high state of combat readiness."

"We shall certainly comply with your instructions."

After Begum Samru had departed, General Rane Khan said to Mahadhji:

"Your dream to have her on your side has been fulfilled. She certainly is very pretty. I have never heard of any woman who is so beautiful, leading a body of fighting soldiers."

It was not long before Begum Samru was called upon to shoulder responsibilities for the defence of the empire.

Finding that Mahadhji was engaged in securing the Emperor's possessions towards the South of the Capital, Ghulam Qadir, the Ruhela Chief and a relation of the Emperor, started eyeing Delhi and the Red Fort. He started moving his troops towards the Capital. Shah Alam, in panic, sent messages to Begum Samru and Mahadhji. The latter was still involved in the operations and could not immediately come to Shah Alam's defence. But the Begum immediately rushed to Delhi with all her battalions and set up her camp near the Fort on the western side of river Yamuna. Meanwhile, Qadir had deployed his forces on the opposite side across the river. Finding Samru's force entrenched in support of the Emperor, the wily Ruhela devised a strategy, hoping to gain his objectives without a serious battle. He sought an interview with the Begum, who agreed to receive him in her camp.

She prepared herself for formal negotiations. The French

commander of her corps furnished her tent elegantly. A beautiful silk carpet was spread on the floor and a magnificent, cushioned chair was placed at the head, with seats for other partakers. But she instructed her commander to keep rigorous watch on Qadir, and on all those accompanying him. Considering his reputation as a scheming crook, she did not want to take any chances.

Begum wore a plain snug turban of embroidered Cashmere, over which a shawl was thrown, enveloping her cheeks, throat, and shoulders; and from the midst of its folds her little grey eyes peered forth with a lynx-like acuteness. Her costume consisted of a short full petticoat, displaying a good deal of her brocade trousers, from under which peeped a pair of embroidered slippers. Her attire met the requirements of modesty and majesty.

As Qadir arrived with a few bodyguards (1787 A.D.), he told the French commander of Samru that he would like to meet her alone, if she had no objection. Begum's officer went in to consult her, he was apprehensive about allowing the visitor to meet her alone. She, however, agreed to talk to him alone, but instructed to keep Qadir's bodyguards at a safe distance. She also advised the officer to train his guns on Qadir's force across the river and be ready to fire at a signal from her. The Frenchman decided to keep a discreet watch on the proceedings through a hole on the rear of the tent.

Qadir had never seen Begum Samru but he had heard a

great deal about her. When he was ushered in, he first offered her the customary salutations. His voice exuded confidence, when he spoke.

"Your Excellency, I bring to you a proposal which can be of mutual interest. You join forces with me and we can share the territories and the wealth of the Emperor who anyway, is quite weak with no ability to defend himself. His Hindu Regent too, is embroiled in his own problems. In any case, we can easily tackle him with the help of many nobles of the court who are opposed to him."

"I am afraid your perception of the Emperor's position is totally misplaced. And, I am here to defend the Emperor and not to stab him in the back." The Begum replied trying to conceal her growing infuriation.

"In fact, I have another greater proposition. Why don't you you marry me? Insha-Allah, you can become the queen empress of Hindustan and both of us will rule from the Red Fort. But if you do not accept my proposal, I advise you to withdraw your force to Sardhana to avoid bloodshed."

Samru Begum could not control herself any longer. She yelled:

"You wily upstart, you have the cheek to aspire to be the King of Delhi. I treat your threats with utter contempt. As far as your insulting proposal is concerned I shall reply to it shortly."

Sensing the commotion, the Frenchman went in. She ordered,

"Escort this man out, and fire a volley of shots at his force as my answer to his proposals."

The Ruhela left the tent in a hurry and rushed across the river. Learning that Mahadhji's force was nearing Delhi, he ordered his troops to withdraw into their own territory.

Shah Alam was gratified to learn that Begum Samru had managed to get rid of the miscreant effectively. He called her to his presence and loaded her with robes of honour and costly gifts. He said:

"Our Empress had told us that on your first visit to her, you had called yourself our slave. You are actually an ornament of your gender. We bestow on you the title of:

Zebun Nissa."

About this time, Samru Begum received through her agents, the copy of a missive written in Farsi by Prince Mirza Jawan Bukht, the eldest son of Shah Alam, addressed to King George III of Great Britain. She thought the contents very explosive, as the prince had implored that the British King direct his governor-general in Calcutta, to go to the aid and assistance of the house of Taimur for the restoration of Mughal authority and their dominions. The prince had written:

'— from the relaxed state of the government and, in consequence of the arrival of the deceitful Marathas, and of Sindhia (who is chief of the seditious) those disturbances and rebellions increasing in tenfold proportion have augmented the distress of our august parent —'

The Begum immediately saw Mahadhji and handed over a copy of the letter. He had a hearty laugh but thanked her profusely for her concern in the matter and promised to make enquiries.

After some time he advised the Begum that the prince had written that letter out of frustration and there was nothing to worry about.

Thomas

Begum Samru, conscious of her additional responsibilities, let it be known all around that she was looking for a new Commander for her troops. George Thomas, an Irish soldier of fortune had arrived in India in a British man-of-war, a short while earlier. After some unsatisfactory assignments in the South of the country, he had made his way to Delhi. He was a tall and sturdy looking man. He approached the Begum for a job. The Begum had always shown a weakness for Europeans, not only in her corps, but even in her personal life. She saw in Thomas, a potential companion. Begum could not resist the temptation to compare, in her mind, Thomas with her late husband; George Thomas was much younger and appeared physically strong and strapping.

Thomas was appointed the new Commander of Sardhana's troops and the civil administrator of the *jagir*. She advised him to find ways and means to increase the income from the territory, as their welfare heavily depended on the revenue from the estate.

Thomas was an energetic and exuberant man. He immersed himself in the management of Sardhana and devised methods to increase the revenue from farming. He initiated schemes to generate revenues from forests within the territory. Observing the considerable movement of various kinds of produce through Sardhana, both from South to North and vice-versa, he proposed to the Begum to levy customs or transit duty on all such traffic. He even proposed transit fees on travellers. Begum was impressed by his acumen, but did not approve of the idea of levying transit fees on travellers.

"Bulk of the passenger traffic through Sardhana comprises of Hindu pilgrims going to Haridwar. I don't want to impose any burden on them." She said.

Appointment of George Thomas triggered off discontent and jealousy among the French officers of Samru's corps who resented a fresh English speaking Irishman, with much lesser experience as their boss. It was widely known that civil responsibilities of George Thomas had brought him much closer to the Begum than any other officer of the corps. The bitterness led to scandal mongering and stories were circulated linking Thomas with the young maids of the Begum.

Soon George Thomas got an opportunity to display his military prowess. One of the feudatories of the Mughal Empire was refusing to remit the tribute due to Shah Alam. He was also harassing the Rajah of Jaipur, who pressed Shah Alam to restrain him. The Shah decided to undertake a military operation on his own, as Mahadhji was busy elsewhere with his troops. Shah Alam asked Begum Samru to accompany him with her battalions.

Emperor with his Mughalia troops and Begum Samru with her entire corps with Thomas in command marched towards Rewari (1788 A.D.). They camped near Gokalgarh with Samru's force on the right of the Emperor. The Royal force intended to attack Najaf Quli, the rebel. However, the rebel force surprised the Mughalia troops, an indisciplined lot, by attacking them at night. The thoroughly demoralised Emperor, on the request of the Begum escaped in a hurry. He took shelter within the square of Begum Samru's infantry.

In the meantime, she sent Najaf Quli, a message, upbraiding him for his conduct and threatening him with immediate and exemplary punishment. She then got into her palanquin, and placed herself at the head of 100 of her own soldiers, accompanied by a six-pounder, commanded by George Thomas. She advanced with this little force, ordered her palanquin to be put down and personally directed a volley from the gun and small fire-arms. Darribere was in the front leading his platoon when a musket shot felled him. Despite his best efforts, Thomas could not save him.

George Thomas then launched his frontal assault on Quli's troops, who retreated under the accurate fire from the Begum's army.

The rebel then recognised, that his only chance was to beg

the Begum to use her considerable influence to secure the Emperor's forgiveness.

"You don't deserve to be pardoned, still I shall talk to the Emperor." The Begum said.

She was determined to crush the rebel, but the Emperor, demoralised with his experience, was in no mood to chase the miscreant. So at Begum Samru's welcome mediation, Shah Alam agreed to patch up a peace treaty.

The Begum presented Najaf Quli to the Emperor, with his wrists tied together with a handkerchief like a penitent captive rebel, to soothe the king's imperial dignity. He also offered to pay certain amount of money to the king. The Emperor forgave his offences and allowed him to continue as heretofore.

Though Shah Alam gained nothing from his latest expedition, he was extremely grateful to Samru Begam for extricating him once again from a precarious position. He showered her with numerous gifts and called her 'his most beloved daughter' in full durbar.

On return to Sardhana, the Begum reflected a good deal on the recent events and felt a tinge of sympathy for the Emperor. She had become quite fond of him. In fact, Shah Alam considered her a member of the family and Prince Akbar Shah, the heir to the throne, treated her as a sister.

She immersed herself in the management of her *jagir*. She realized with pleasure that under efficient administration, her income was multiplying manifold. She was grateful to Thomas for ensuring discipline in Sardhana peasantry and for effectively controlling her revenue officials. His military skills were equally good, as the Begum found out from the battle against Najaf Quli at Gokulgarh.

One day when George Thomas came to discuss some urgent financial matters with the Begum, he found her crying inconsolably.

Alarmed he asked her, "What is bothering you?"

"I have just now received reliable and confidential information that Ghulam Qadir gained admittance with a force of two thousand men in the Red Fort. There is a group of guards called the Red Brigade at the entrance of the fort. But Nazir, the Superintendent of the palace, proved to be treacherous. He advised the guards to allow Qadir's men undisturbed admission to the palace."

She went on, sobbing.

"You can well imagine what followed. He forced the Emperor to give him the post of Regent and Mir- Bakhshi (Commander-in Chief) of the Empire, feigning undying loyalty to the House of Taimur by swearing on Quran and bowing down to him that his head touched the feet of the Emperor.

Immediately after, he went on to humiliate Shah Alam and inflict all possible indignities and torture on the women of the harem. He wanted to know about the treasure house of the Emperor. And when he was told that there is no money in the palace, he had the audacity to physically belabour Shah Alam and disrobe the princesses and use foul language. He even insulted the *mallika*. Qadir got so insane with rage at not being able to locate the fabled wealth of the king, that he ultimately blinded the Emperor by pulling out his eyes with his own hands. (August 1788 A.D.) And then he declared Bidar Bakht, a distant relation of Shah Alam, as the Emperor, and put Shah Alam and his entire family in dungeons within the fort."

"Oh! My God, why did the Emperor not inform Rane Khan or us? I am sure, I would have been able to tackle that rascal." Thomas was shaken by the Begum's account.

"I am quite sure of that. But the *Nazir* blocked all communication to the outside world. I feel so frustrated."

The Begum started crying again. Thomas took her in his arms to console her and planted a kiss on her lips. The Begum melted in his arms.

"Our immediate task is to hunt down that scoundrel. Crying won't help. The Emperor is very fond of you, why don't you go to meet him and try to help him in his hour of misery." Thomas suggested.

"Please get in touch with Rane Khan and ask him how can we help in tracking down Qadir. I will go to meet Shah Alam once the efforts to capture that criminal is started in right earnest. No body wants to be seen in a state of such misery, and then, he is the Emperor. Do arrange for at least one *maund* of high quality opium. I will present it to the King when I go to meet him. You know how fond he is of opium."

Elegy

After a short while Mahadhji's General Rane Khan was able to apprehend the ruffian, with the assistance of Samru's corps. He was put in an iron cage, specially made for the purpose and suspended on a rope in front of the army. Soldiers heaped all kinds of insults and indignities on the prisoner. Before killing him, Qadir's eyes were scooped out as desired by Shah Alam and sent to him in a casket, to satisfy the kings's thirst for revenge. Qadir's accomplice, Nazir was trodden to death under the feet of an elephant.

Khutba was read from the Jama Masjid in the name of the restored Emperor. Mahadhji continued to be the Regent. To express his gratitude, Shah Alam handed over the governance of the Hindu holy cities of Mathura and Brindavan to Mahadhji. In addition, he banned cow slaughter in deference to the sentiments of his Hindu subjects.

Though Shah Alam got back his throne, he could not regain his jewellery that Qadir looted from the royal palace. Lesteneau, a French officer of Rane Khan's army, had captured Qadir's saddlebags stuffed with looted jewels and diamonds. But he kept the knowledge of the catch a secret and on returning to Agra, drew his soldier's pay from Sindhia, and escaped to Europe with all that cash and the royal jewellery. The fact came to light only after the Frenchman was out of reach.

Begum Samru went to the Red Fort and first went to see the *mallika*.

"Come Zebun-Nissa, I have been wanting to meet you."

The Queen embraced her, crying.

"The King had been remembering you all the time. If Zebun-Nissa were here, this misfortune would not have befallen us, he had said. You cannot imagine what that fiend did to us. It was as if he derived immense pleasure in inflicting pain to his Majesty. He threatened the sovereign that if he did not disclose where our treasures were kept, he would dig out his eyes. The Emperor retorted whether he would destroy those eyes that have been assiduously employed in perusing the sacred Quran for over sixty years now. But that had no effect on the rascal. He threw his Majesty on the floor and climbed over his bososm and pierced both his eyes with a piognard."

Samru Begum burst into tears hearing this horrid tale.

"*Mallika* Zamani and Sahiba Mahal, widows of the late king Muhammad Shah were hand in glove with the devil. There was treason everywhere."

"Why should they do it?"

'They wanted to depose his majesty and make Bidar Bakht, their grand son, the king. He demanded twelve lakh rupees for this service and the women managed to give him the amount."

"Hai Allah!"

"Bidar Bakht was given possession of the palace and the Fort, and his majesty, was confined in the Moti masjid, the small mosque within the Fort. The fiend subjected the royal family to gross dishonour and suffering. I was personally saved from disgrace by Maniar Singh, a Jat companion of Qadir."

"I really wish you had found some way to inform me."

"Once Qadir's soldiers occupied the Fort with the help of the *Nazir*, they blocked all communications with the outside world, and looted our jewels, diamonds and cash. They starved tender children and helpless women to death by denying food and water for days together. They put all the princes and male members of the royal house in the dungeons in the Fort. When Mahadhji's general rescued them after eight weeks of incarceration, they looked like living skeletons and had long nails and unshorn dirty beards and long hair. They appeared like denizens of a jungle."

"I have detained you far too long, his majesty will be happy to meet you. Let us go to him."

Begum Samru called one of her attendants, who brought in a wooden box. The queen said,

"What is it?"

"Opium, for his Majesty."

"It is very thoughtful of you. In his present state, it would be of much use to him."

As the two ladies went to meet the King, the *mallika* said,

"Your Majesty! Zebun-Nissa has come to meet you."

"Bring her near me, I want to touch her."

As Begum Samru went close to Shah Alam, he held her face in his palms. He said in a quivering voice:

"If you were here, that rascal would not have dared to touch us."

"It is my misfortune that I could not be of assistance to your Majesty, in your hour of need."

Begum Samru presented the box of opium to Shah Alam and vowed fidelity to the house of Taimur till her last breath.

As a mark of his affection and gratitude to Zebun-Nissa, Shah Alam granted the *jagir* of Badshahpur Jharsa to Zafaryab Khan, her step-son. Begum Samru had requested this favour much earlier. She had also requested for the title of nawab for her stepson. This wish too was granted.

When the Begum was about to leave, the *mallika* gave her a piece of paper with a text written in Farsi. Mallika explained that it was an elegy composed by the Emperor after the loss of his sight

When Begum Samru reached Sardhana, she lay down in her bed and started reading the long composition. She broke down when she read the first few lines.

> Where with bright pomp the stately domes arise,
> In yon dark tower an aged monarch lies,
> Forlorn, dejected, blind, replete with woes,
> In tears his august aspect shews

> Time was, O King, when clothed in power supreme,
> Thy voice was heard, and nations hailed the theme;
> Now sad reverse, for sordid lust of gold,
> By traitorous wiles, thy throne and empire sold.'

> Chaste partners of my bed, and joys serene,
> Once my delight, but now how changed the scene!
> Condemned with me in plaintive strains to mourn.'

> 'Thee, O Sindhia, illustrious chief,
> Who once didst promise to afford relief
> Thee I invoke, exert thy generous aid,
> And over their heads high, wave the avenging blade.'

The poignant poerty ran into many pages.

Razia

Meanwhile, Gulbadan noticed that Farzana had started getting too fond of Thomas. But there was a queer twist. After Darribere's death at Gokalgarh, Nooro too had grown close to the charming, sturdy Irishman. It was a very unusual situation. Farzana was nearing forty and her daughter was less than half her age, and both had become admirers of the same man. Gulbadan was reminded of her first love, which Nur Bai had stopped in its tracks. She still remembered the twinge of Nur Bai's slap.

'I was all fire when first I fell in love;

Now at the last nothing but ash remains.'

Gulbadan sighed deeply.

She had a premonition that in the present scenario nothing good could come out for the Begum. The rivalry and jealousy between the mother and daughter could only lead to disaster. Could the foreigner keep both the mother and daughter happy in his harem? That would be unprecedented.

Gulbadan deliberated on the issue and decided to talk to Farzana.

"I want to talk to you on an urgent matter. Farzo! I find that you are growing too fond of George Thomas."

"I certainly like him."

"Do you want to be his mistress or have a *nikah* with him?"

"He has already proposed to me. As both of us are Christians, we shall get married in Agra church. But, that would be after sometime. As of now, I do not want to think too much about it. We shall wait till the impact of the tragedy in the Red Fort subsides a little." The Begum disclosed her plans.

"Somehow, I feel that he wants to marry you because of your *jagir* and the steady income that comes with it. Once he marries you, he will become the master of your corps. A foreign mercenary can hope for nothing better than to own the finest fighting force in Hindustan, and a pretty wife like you." Gulbadan thought her words would compel the Begum to have second thoughts. "Long time back when you first called on the *mallika*, you told me that she called you a modern day Razia Sultana. I wonder if you know the full story of Razia. This happened 500 years ago. After a very successful reign of four years at Delhi she developed a clandestine liaison with a young Abyssinian employee. There was large scale resentment in her army and she was elbowed aside by a junta from amongst her nobility."

To add a tinge of jealousy in Farzana's mind, Gulbadan added,

"Thomas is much younger to you, he is only 32 and naturally, he is chasing young girls around here."

"Who has the audacity to snatch him away from me? I shall not spare her."

"Please bear in mind the effect all this will have on your corps; you are so much attached to it. I am afraid any emotional involvement with a subordinate will create indiscipline in the corps. Already there is enough resentment."

After the tragedy at the Red Fort, the Begum felt increasingly insecure. She became edgy and worked up. To soothe her nerves, she took to smoking a hookah and had it carried wherever she went.

Her frame of mind exhibited itself in a tragic way.

One day the Begum happened to see a slave girl kissing George Thomas passionately in an obscure corner of the house. She was furious. She called the girl to her office and had her beaten up mercilessly till she died. Nonchalantly, she had a hole dug in the room and body buried in it. The floor was covered and the Begum sat above the grave unconcernedly, smoking her hookah as if the whole affair was a trifling occurrence. This incident sent shock waves through the corps. Gulbadan was extremely upset and was convinced that Farzana had lost her balance, she was now seriously concerned about her future.

In 1790, a flamboyant Frenchman, Le Vassoult joined Samru's corps as an officer. He had the manners and deportment of a man of good birth, though of a haughty disposition. He was a cavalier of sorts. This personable young Frenchman swept the Begum off her feet. He would talk to her about his country and compared her with the great Joan of Arc. This tickled her vanity. Gradually, Thomas went out of favour in the Begum's mind.

One day, the French officer went to her office to discuss some urgent problems. She was smoking her hookah and poring over some papers in her study. Le Vassoult, dressed in the commander's uniform, entered the room and saluted her.

"Your highness, I am sorry to disturb you at this hour but the matter is so urgent, it brooks no delay."

"I am feeling rather concerned, please say what it is."

"The German officer, Schulanberg, who is close to Thomas is trying to spread disaffection in his unit under Thomas's guidance. He has to be dismissed from service."

"My information is that there is some restlessness among a section of the troops, because of our friendship. Some of them think that I am being disloyal to the hallowed memory of my first husband, who founded the corps. I think once we get married there should be no problem."

"But I do feel that the German fellow must be removed forthwith."

"It is better not to precipitate matters at this stage, as it might lead to more disturbances."

She moved to the sofa in the corner of her study. Sensing that Le Vassoult was disappointed at her decision and was sulking, she invited him to sit next to her. She took out a bottle of claret and two glasses from a cupboard.

"You deserve some wine after your anxious moments about that German. We must learn to relax once in a while."

Le Vassoult loosened after a couple of glasses of wine. The Begum was also enjoying her drink. She said playfully:

"Come on, let us see you smile. You look even more handsome when you are cheerful."

He beamed and held her hand. She turned her face towards him and he kissed her. The Begum was not protesting and he put his tongue deep in her mouth. He pulled her to the floor, and whispered:

"It would give an added kick if the commander, in his uniform, lays his supreme commander in her office."

She laughed out.

The illicit encounters became frequent and it came to be widely discussed, leading to consternation among the devoted admirers of her late husband Reinhardt.

Le Vassoult became the unrivalled adviser of the Begum.

"In France, the nobility moves about in horse drawn carriages. That is more dignified than travelling in bullock carts and of course, faster and more comfortable." He said once.

"Why don't you make such a carriage for me?"

In a short period of time, Le Vassoult fabricated a beautiful coach. He trained four horses, which could pull the coach; he explained that two were intended to be stand-bys. Two people were trained as coachmen. When the coach was all set, the Begum went for a drive, with Le Vassoult sitting by her side. The horse drawn coach was quite a sensation in Sardhana.

And the Begum got all the more besotted.

Le Vassoult

The Begum was piqued that George Thomas preferred younger women. In any case, she had acquired a new beau-ideal. She did not want to have anything further to do with George Thomas in her personal life. She showed decided preference for the Frenchman over Thomas. This led to animosity between the two officers and factious partisanship among the soldiers.

Gulbadan had foreseen this possibility and remonstrated with Farzana.

"I told you only the first part of Razia's story. There is a sequel. There was revolt at Bhatinda in the Punjab in high summer. Bravely she dashed across, but was isolated by the conspirators who killed her Abyssinian friend. She ended up as a prisoner in the fort, which she had gone to redeem. There she managed to win the backing and affection of one of the conspirators. They were married and gathering further support, marched on to Delhi. But they were defeated, and while fleeing from the battle-field, they were caught and killed. I only wanted to emphasize that if a woman ruler, who is single, allows flutters of heart to sway her decisions, only disaster will result."

But the Begum would not relent, and was determined to marry Le Vassoult. The blind Emperor at Delhi, immersed though he was in his own misfortunes, learnt of the latest developments in Sardhana through his informers and was seriously concerned about Begum Samru's resolve to marry the French officer. He called the Begum to his presence to clarify what he had heard.

"I gathered that George Thomas, the gallant young man who saved the day against Najaf Kuli at Gokalgarh, is out of your favour now. And that you intend to marry a Frenchman, is that right?"

"Yes, your Majesty."

"What has happened to your fabled sagacity and common sense? Do you realise that any such step will seriously affect your standing in your corps? There will be intrigues and indiscipline. I strongly urge you to desist from undertaking any such step. I am advising you only because I consider you as my daughter."

"I know your Majesty is genuinely interested in my welfare, but I can assure you that I will overcome the problems you are anticipating."

The Emperor was disappointed but he could not do anything further. He bade farewell to Begum Samru and wished her all the best.

The Frenchman was now determined to undermine the influence of his rival. He instigated a few French officers of Sardhana corps to circulate rumours that Thomas was planning a rebellion against the Begum.

Thomas was dismayed and disgusted with these developments. He resigned from the service but refused to vacate Tappal, his headquarters located within Sardhana. Begum Samru lost all sense of proportion and was bent upon destroying Thomas. She planned a march towards Tappal with her battalions, twenty guns and four squadrons. Many officers of the corps tried in vain to dissuade her from this suicidal step.

Gulbadan was seriously alarmed. She felt that between the two European suitors of the Begum, Thomas was better not only as a soldier but as a human being as well. She accepted that the Frenchman was bit of a dandy, and Thomas was rather ungainly but that was no reason why the Begum should compromise her future and security. She had felt even earlier from the days when she was a courtesan, that she was willful and sneaky. She felt guilty that she had sowed the seeds of suspicion in the Begum's heart against Thomas. But at least the mother and daughter would not clash with each other over a common lover.

Gulbadan was now equally concerned about Nooro. She was to be married off. She talked to the Begum about this.

"Why don't you look for a groom and let me know." She said.

"I hear you intend to undertake a military operation against George to evict him from Tappal. I don't think it is a wise decision. We don't want a conflict between the French and the English in our backyard. That could embroil us in the power struggle of the two European countries. Allow me to meet him, I might be able to convince him to leave peacefully."

Begum Samru agreed.

Gulbadan went to meet Thomas.

"Why haven't you married yet?"

"I thought you knew the reason. I wanted to marry Begum Samru and she was also keen and had assured me that we would get married in the church at Agra after some time once the impact of the tragedy in the Red Fort softened. But then this Frenchman appears on the scene and she takes a somersault. And that French fellow initiates intrigues against me, out of jealousy, I presume."

"I am sure you still like the Begum, and that you are her wellwisher. You will realize that marriage with her is impossible now. If you agree, I can look for a suitable young girl for you."

"I am flattered by your interest in my wellbeing. I shall welcome any steps that you may take in this matter."

"But you should give me some time. Do not take any hasty measures. And, do vacate Tappal; you are so well known that you can be accommodated by any of the good chiefs."

"I shall vacate Tappal as soon as I can make an alternative

arrangement for my sustenance."

Gulbadan conveyed the gist of her dialogue with Thomas to the Begum and told her about her plans to give Nooro in marriage to Thomas. Within a short time, Thomas received an offer from a Maratha chief.

Bliss

George Thomas vacated Tappal and took up service with Appa Khandi Rao. There was considerable resentment within the corps at the treatment meted out to Thomas. But her infatuation with the Frenchman grew stronger by the moment.

In 1793, the Begum sent a message to Father Gregorio who had baptised her twelve years earlier at Agra, intimating him her intention to get married to Le Vassoult in the church.

Father Gregorio was quite excited and honoured by this message. He wrote back to her:

'Your Excellency, we, the Christians in Agra, feel extremely happy for you. We would be delighted to take part in the marriage ceremony and would love to host a reception thereafter. I wonder if you are aware of the fact that the Christians here are very proud of you, you being the only Christian Chief in the whole of Hindustan.'

Their marriage was an elaborate and magnificent affair. The couple was invited to different homes but the Frenchman was ill at ease in these gatherings, much to the surprise of Samru Begum. On the advice Father Gregorio, the Begum took advantage of the occasion to add the name 'Nobilis' to her Christian appellation.

To celebrate the marriage, the Christians of Agra held a grand reception for the bride and groom in a *shamiana* near the famous mausoleum of Mumtaz Mahal, built by Emperor Shahjahan on the banks of river Yamuna for the memory of his favourite wife. After a sumptuous dinner, a dance performance was organized in the honour of guests, the mausoleum glittering in moonlight providing the backdrop. Begum Samru was reminded of her earlier life as a *nautch* girl. She reflected on her fate and realised that she could not have met and married Reinhardt, her late husband if she had not been a dancer in Nur Bai's haveli.

On return to Sardhana, the Begum's husband moved to her bungalow on her request. Gulbadan had an instant dislike for the man. But the Begum was in the seventh heaven, floating in the clouds, in absolute bliss and ecstasy. Gulbadan didn't feel comfortable in Sardhana anymore. She wanted to get away for a change.

Gulbadan learnt that a major Kumbh *mela* was to be held at Haridwar. This congregation of pilgrims was held only after an interval of twelve years where hundreds of thousands of people from far off places like Bengal, Gujarat, Kashmir and Punjab would gather for the sacred bath in the Ganga at

Haridwar. She had a personal agenda as well. She had heard that *Pandas* of Haridwar maintained family history of different pilgrims according to their castes and hometowns. Gulbadan vaguely remembered visiting the holy town with her parents just before her world turned upside down. She wanted to learn something more about her family.

"A Kumbh *mela* is going to be held at Haridwar in near future. As you know this occasion comes only once in twelve years. I would like to go and spend a few days at Haridwar and Rishikesh. And if you don't mind, I would like to take Nooro with me. It should be an interesting experience for her." Gulbadan expressed her wish.

The Begum was too happy to agree. She felt a little inhibited with Gulbadan and Nooro around. She detailed a small detachment from amongst her corps to escort them to Haridwar.

Haridwar

The tents for Nooro and Gulbadan were pitched on the banks of Ganga, near a small village called Kankhal, a little downstream of the sacred *ghats* at Haridwar. The crowds of pilgrims were building up day by day.

Gulbadan and Nooro would walk along the river and go up to the *ghats* to watch the crowds of pilgrims in myriad coloured dresses speaking totally unintelligible languages. As they walked, cool refreshing breeze would waft in from the mountains. The great *ghats* had some sixty steps and were about one hundred feet in width, reaching down to the edge of the Ganga. This was the holiest spot in Haridwar and was most part of the day thronged by hundreds of men, women and children, some descending for the holy dip and others attempting to climb up in the dripping garments. Nooro's wandering eyes lingered on young men in their loincloths.

About 500 or more people of both sexes and all ages, dipped in the holy water at the same moment. The men, particularly the elderly of them, were occupied offering prayers while the women were mostly laughing and chattering and enjoying themselves.

At the great *ghats,* in the evenings many pilgrims would place little clay *diyas* in cups made of dried leaves of *peepul* in the river, with prayers on their lips. The lighted diyas floating down the river looked ethereal.

At night, all the tents and booths were illuminated, and the scene was hardly less animated by night than by day, but what struck Gulbadan the most was the reigning order and tranquility despite a massive congregation of pilgrims and traders flocking the place. She found it extraordinary that women and children felt entirely safe and secure in the midst of a hundred thousand people, all strangers to each other.

A large number of *sadhus* from different regions had also assembled there. Many of them had come down from their abodes in the mountains in the North; the pilgrims held them in great esteem. Some of these *sadhus* wore no clothes and moved about naked.

Gulbadan asked one of the escorts to locate the concerned family *panda* and invite him to meet her in her tent. The panda duly reported expecting a good contribution. She told him that her father was a wellknown astrologer who had important nobles as his clients and that her parents had visited Haridwar before Nadir Shah's invasion. He was killed in the mass slaughter ordered by Nadir Shah and her mother was taken a captive.

The panda wanted to know her father's name.

Gulbadan shook her head. "I am afraid I do not know. Could you try to identify our family from what I have told you?"

The next day the panda came over and read out the entries in his ledger:

"Pandit Ram Shastri *raj-jyotishi*, son of Pandit Bhagrith Das, resident of Neel Katra of Delhi, arrived at Haridwar on fourteenth of September 1738 for a holy dip in the Ganga accompanied by his wife named Rukmini and a little girl child called Bharti." The account also stated that an offering of one silver rupee was made to the panda.

Gulbadan had no means to verify the record but she accepted it.

As the auspicious day ior a dip in Ganga drew closer, a veritable bazar, a grand commercial emporium for selling of merchandise, sprung up. Horses, camels, bullocks, dry fruits, zaffron and shawls from Kashmere were all there to tempt the pilgrims from distant lands. Textiles from the Punjab were a great draw.

The inhabitants of surrounding villages benefited tremendously from the pilgrims. They brought business to their petty shops. The pilgrims were expected to pay a small tax to the *chowkidars*. Offerings were made to the Brahmans responsible for the maintenance of temples and shrines.

The Marathas imposed a whole lot of taxes on the pilgrims.

Eight annas were charged for each horse as well as for each wheeled carriage, brought to the fair. Camel owners had to pay six annas for each animal. Two annas were charged for each palanquin.

Nooro said to Gulbadan:

"I have been wondering all this while, how people of different regions, speaking different languages, separated by hundreds of miles congregate at the same time at Haridwar?"

"The Brahmans issue a calendar of auspicious fares and festivals well in advance in the language of the region. Kumbh melas at Haridwar and Kashi are the most popular with the pilgrims attracting very large crowds, despite the difficulties and risks of long distance travel." Gulbadan explained.

After a few days, Nooro and Gulbadan returned to Sardhana, refreshed and happy. In the meantime, realities of life were slowly dawning upon Samru Begum.

Nemesis

The ecstasy of Begum's marriage was rather short lived. Le Vassoult was totally devoid of tact. He could not communicate effectively with his subordinates in the corps, for want of proper command over Urdu or Farsi nor could he speak fluent English.

Soon after marriage, the Frenchman started throwing his weight about among the corps and the revenue officials of Sardhana. He was arrogant and haughty, and soon repelled officers and soldiers of the corps with his overbearing and insolent behaviour. He harassed any officer who was supposed to be close to Thomas. A French officer, who was very popular with the troops and was known to be close to Thomas, specially attracted his hostile attention. Le Vassoult demoted the French officer, generating antipathy. Some officers conspired together and decided to overthrow the Begum and her husband.

The Begum was alarmed at these developments, and tried to restrain her husband. She advised him to respect the sensibilities of other officers but he would not listen to her.

He even considered sharing his dining table with other officers below his prestige and looked down on them as the riff-raff of European society.

Gulbadan's account of Razia Sultana began to haunt the Begum. She didn't want to commit the same mistake; she didn't want to lose control of her corps. Between the corps and her husband, she would any day prefer the former. The corps was her first love.

The conspiracy assumed serious proportions. The conspirators wanted to place Zafaryab Khan, son of the late Reinhardt Sombre, in command of the corps. Zafaryab did not accept the dangerous honour readily, as he was quite skeptical what would come out of it. But at last, on the assurance of some officers and soldiers, he consented to their proposal.

The revolt within the corps was so sweeping that both the Begum and her husband were genuinely worried about their lives. They entered into a mutual pact, that neither would survive the other, in case the mutineers killed one of them. They at once took to flight, hoping to get refuge in Awadh. Their plans were leaked out to Zafaryab, who sent a party of cavalry to intercept them. The cavalry surrounded the Begum in her palanquin, only four miles from Sardhana. Zafaryab proclaimed free pardon to a few armed attendants with the Begum, provided they would give her up and her husband, who had ridden ahead.

Sitting in her palanquin, held aloft by her bearers, she espied Ghasi Ram, a *subeda*r of the corps who she knew well. She peremptorily ordered, on the top of her voice:

"Ghasi Ram! Come here."

He ran to up to the palanquin and saluted her.

"*Huzoo*r?"

"You have eaten our salt. All of you of my corps have received the best of every thing amongst all the private armies of Hindustan. You enjoy the highest *izzat-o-iqbal* in the whole country. What does this non-sense mean?"

"I am only carrying out the orders of my seniors."

"And what are their orders?"

"To arrest you and deliver you to Zafaryab Khan along with your husband."

The Begum was incensed at the reply of the *subedar* and shouted,

"You want to kill us? Rather than be humiliated and killed by the faithless mutineers, we shall die by our own hands."

The Begum drew her bejewelled dagger, which she always carried with her, and struck it across her breast. Blood gushed out.

There was a general tumult all around, and someone cried out,

"The Begum has killed herself."

Le Vassoult, who had ridden ahead on his horse, looked

back. He saw blood dripping down from the palanquin.

"What has happened?" He yelled.

Soldiers shouted in one voice,

"Begum Samru has killed herself."

Le Vassoult could not believe his ears. But as per his compact with the Begum before their flight, he took out his pistol, put it in his mouth and pulled the trigger. Le Vassoult sprang a foot into the air as the shot struck him, before falling down, dead. His death failed to evoke any sympathy among the corps. The dead body was kicked and dragged about before they threw it in a ditch (1795 A.D.)

The Begum was conducted back to Sardhana as a prisoner. Her wound was not serious and she recovered fast.

Confined to a small cell under tight security, Begum Samru had plenty of time to reflect on her foibles and follies. She realised that her predilection for being generous with her favours to Europeans was one of the reasons for her downfall. She admitted to herself that after her satisfactory and successful marriage with Walter, she was enamoured of the Europeans who came in contact with her, whether it be Thomas, or the French officer Montigny who was an aspirant for her hand before Thomas, or the flamboyant Le Vassoult. She felt that she had betrayed the trust, which her wellwishers had reposed in her. In short, her dalliance with numerous lovers was her undoing and nemesis had overtaken her.

Gulbadan was relieved that Farzana had recovered from her

114

self-inflicted injury. On her request, she was allowed to see Samru in captivity. Seeing her, Gulbadan started crying. She said to Samru:

"We must not lose heart, but try to get out of this deplorable situation of our own making. Shah Alam, I understand, is greatly perturbed at your incarceration, but after the death of General Rane Khan earlier and more recently, of Mahadji, he feels helpless and worried about his own safety. Now the only person, who can perhaps help, is George Thomas. But the way you treated him and tried to destroy him, I am not sure if he would come to our rescue. But there is no harm in appealing to him for help, after all, he is still your well-wisher."

"Amma! I realise that I was extremely unfair to George. Looking back, I feel that I have committed numerous mistakes. If I get back my *jagir*, I promise that I shall conduct myself in a more responsible and just manner. But tell me, why is Zafaryab so hostile to me?"

"Well, it is not at all surprising. He is the only son of his late father, the rich and wealthy Walter Reinhardt Sombre. But he has largely been kept out of the rich legacy of his father. You remember that he was very keen to take over the corps and Sardhana soon after the demise of his father. He feels aggrieved and is trying to obtain what he feels should legitimately belong to him."

"But he was totally unfit to handle any responsible position. Anyway, the Emperor will never transfer the *jagir* to any body else now and the corps too will disintegrate without any means of maintenance. And then, it was on my request that the Emperor granted the *jagir* of Badshahpur Jharsa to Zafaryab and conferred him the title of Nawab, though the worthy Nawab could not manage even that small estate. I had to look after his *jagir* too. I have improved farming in his *jagir* and enhanced the revenue."

"I know Farzo, but it would have been better to maintain friendly relations with your stepson. You could have invited his wife Juliana, their daughter Julia Anne and his mother to stay with you."

"I did consider that but I was not sure of his loyalty. I thought he might indulge in intrigue against me. Any way, if I get my *jagir* back I shall invite Zafaryab and his family to stay with me and look after them."

The setbacks in her life had made the Begum, sober, wiser.

Rescue

Gulbadan was relieved that Farzana was rid of the self-imposed fetters that her imprudent marriage had landed her in. She had a suspicion that Farzana had stage-managed the unusual drama to get rid of her French husband. George Thomas was quite certain that the Begum had indulged in her usual chicanery, to free herself from the liability, which her husband had turned out to be. Nevertheless, George was happy at the sordid exit of his erstwhile rival.

The Begum decided to seek the help of George Thomas as per Gulbadan's advice. She was nervous and drew up several drafts. Finally she sent him a letter.

My dear George,

You can well imagine the pain and humiliation that I am undergoing at present, mainly due to my own folly. I did not follow your advice in the management of my affairs. Now I am completely defeated. I have lost the corps, my peace of mind and a genuine and reliable friend like you. I remember the excellent relationship that we had in official and personal life. Even his Majesty had reminded me of your achievements at Gokalgarh.

My only hope to retrieve the situation lies with you. I am confident that you will rescue me from this agony.

I shall, of course meet all the expenses that may be incurred for any military operation.

With prayers for your happiness and well being

Yours affectionately

Zebun-Nissa.

George Thomas couldn't help smiling to himself when he read the letter and set about the task of helping Begum Samru. He got in touch with his employer Appa Khandi Rao and persuaded him to lend a helping hand, assuring him that the Begum would make adequate payment.

Thomas made an announcement through beat of the drum that Begum Samru continued to be the lawful authority in Sardhana and if any body were to resist her authority he would be severely punished. He discussed the matter with the officers of the corps as well.

"If the Begum should die, under the torture of mind and body to which you are subjecting her, the Emperor will very soon resume the lands assigned for your payment, and disband a force so disorderly and so little likely to be of any use to the Emperor." He told them.

He induced some of his old associates of Sardhana corps,

on promise of reward, to arrest the usurper and to reinstate the Begum. The Begum was restored but there was a counter-revolution. Zafaryab ordered an attack on Thomas, who had come on the scene with a limited force. But additional troops of Thomas arrived just in time and the mutineers had to surrender themselves.

The Begum was formally reinstated and under the supervision of Thomas, oaths of allegiance were administered. Zafaryab was plundered and taken prisoner. He was shifted to Delhi and confined there, where he resumed his passtime of writing Urdu poetry. He abandoned all hopes of getting any share of his father's legacy.

Soon after regaining her *jagir*, the Begum adopted a seal with the name 'Joanna Nobilis Somer'. She was always grateful to her first husband for bequeathing the Sardhana corps to her and therby, giving her the present social rank. It was natural for her to perpetuate his memory by incorporating part of his name in her seal.

Chastisement

Mahadji had died, after a prolonged illness that had caused him lot of pain and trauma. He believed that his enemies had brought about this ailment upon him by black magic. He sought the help of *pandits* and *pujaris* to exorcise the effect of black magic but to no avail. During the period of his illness, the governance of the empire suffered a good deal. But with his departure from the scene, the situation became rather dismal.

The developing uncertainties caused considerable anxiety to the Begum. She also learnt that General Perron of Sindhia and Ambaji, a subordinate Maratha chief, had designs on her *jagir*. She set about taking pre-emptive action to secure her position by getting in touch with the Sikh chiefs in the North. She sought the support of Thomas too. But still, General Perron initiated hostile moves against the Begum.

Thomas strongly remonstrated with Perron for his intrigues against the Begum. She also moved some troops as a display of force. The upshot of her various steps was that Mahadhji's successor Daulat Rao chastised Perron, and advised him to desist from harassing their old ally. In fact, Sindhia instructed his General to personally call upon the lady and apologise to her.

When the General met the Begum, she said,

"I am very disappointed with your behaviour. Surely, you ought to have been aware of my standing with the Emperor as well as the late Regent. You thought I was ineffective in issues of governance due to my personal problems and you could ride roughshod over my interests."

"I have come to express my sincere and profound regrets. I have to assure you on behalf of Sindhia, that you continue to enjoy his full confidence and support as a valuable ally. He also asked me to assure you that he will be ever watchful of your interests."

"I am sure you have behaved the way you did as I did not allow you to be a part of my corps when you begged for it, before you joined the Sindhias. Your behaviour only confirms that my judgement was sound. I am really surprised that they selected you, to succeed so outstanding a general as De-Boigne, who after his return to France, has become a close confidant of Napoleon. I am certain if you were to try to contact Napoleon, when you return to your country, he would throw you out."

After the tongue lashing by the Begum, Perron departed thoroughly demoralized and feeling very foolish.

Haryana

Gulbadan now proceeded with her scheme to marry off Nooro to George Thomas. She wished that the marriage had taken place earlier but the catastrophe that ensued Begum's marriage with Le Vassoult had disturbed all her plans.

She sent a message to Thomas to meet her at an early opportunity. He was busy with his military campaign in Haryana on behalf of the Maratha chief, so he could come only after a few months. When he heard her proposal, he said,

"I am delighted and honoured. I understand she is the daughter of Begum Samru herself but was brought up by you."

"I do not want to comment on that. But if you agree to marry her, you will not call yourself a relation of the Begum."

"I am quite capable of looking after myself and my family, without any claim of any kind on the Begum. By the way, does Nooro know about this bit of her past?"

"I doubt very much."

Soon after, Thomas married Nooro as per Christian rites at a private ceremony. Begum Samru did not attend the function.

Thomas took his newly wedded wife to Georgegarh Fort, which he had built to facilitate his military operations. A powerful troop guarded the fort. Nooro was surprised at the desert like terrain, and the dry condition of the country and felt Sardhana was a much better place.

They talked to each other in Farsi. Thomas explained to Nooro that he intended to set up an independent principality of his own.

"Isn't that being very ambitious?" Nooro was doubtful.

Thomas was, however, certain in his mind.

"The country of Haryana, for many years, did not acknowledge any master. The troubled state of this territory, at present, offers the best opportunity to any determined soldier to grab the country. But my vision extends far beyond setting my own principality. I have dreams of conquering the Punjab and ultimately planting the British flag at Attock for my King and my country."

"I think it is an unrealistic dream."

He tried to explain himself further.

"Since I started serving the Indian chiefs in Hindustan, I have had a rather frustrating experience. At first, I joined Begum Samru. I was completely devoted to her. Even Shah Alam was grateful to me when I extricated him from a very precarious situation at Gokalgarh, not far from here. Begum's stock with the Emperor really rose after that incident. And yet, mark you, she tried to evict me from Sardhana by force, before her marriage with Le Vassoult. I rescued her when her stepson engineered a rebellion in her corps and made her a prisoner. In fact, I personally reinstated her at Sardhana."

"I am really surprised at this lack of gratitude."

"I then joined Appa Khandi Rao. He asked me to reduce Mewat area where villages were not paying their dues to him. I forced them to behave and they paid up all the arrears. Some time after that Appa's soldiers mutinied. His life was in danger and he sent me frantic messages to help him. Despite severe rainstorm I rushed to his aid and brought out Appa and his family to a safe place. He called me his son, and gave me some additional area as *jagir*. He even authorised additional troops for my force. And yet, he became jealous of my military success and intrigued against me."

"I never knew that people could be this vicious."

"You have not heard all. Not long afterwards, Appa died and I rather foolishly accepted employment with Appa's son, Waman Rao, who succeeded him as the chief. This fellow lacked average common sense and felt threatened because of my force. He conspired with Perron, Sindhia's General to destroy me. It was with great difficulty, that I broke through the army of my enemies and got to Hansi, my fort in the North. Thereafter, I strengthened my position, so that my opponents were more hesitant to harass me. I have grown rich plundering my enemies. Can you blame me for wanting to have an independent principality after all these harrowing experiences I underwent?"

Nooro kept quiet. She understood Thomas' feelings. Gradually, she became an ardent admirer of her husband, as she observed the devotion of his soldiers to their commander. Many of them talked to her about the unparalleled heroism and military skill of Thomas. She concluded that her husband was a born leader of men.

Thomas took his wife to Hansi, which he had made his capital. The fortress was situated at a height and looked quite imposing and was said to be impenetrable. As they approached the fort, Thomas explained to Nooro that the fort had come into his possession after a determined struggle against the petty Rajah, who owned it earlier. He had now got it repaired and modified.

Nooro liked the bungalow situated on the banks of the Umtee tank. This was her home now. There was a fort around it, to ensure security. Nooro compared her bungalow with the Begum's house in Sardhana, which she certainly found more elegant, with green lawns and garden. Hansi was set in the middle of a desert with limited access to water.

Thomas took Nooro around the fort. He showed her the mint where he coined his own money. This really surprised her – she could not imagine that the chiefs could mint their own money. Thomas also showed her his factories, where he cast his own artillery, made matchlocks and muskets. He also made his own gunpowder and munitions of war. It was clear to Nooro that Thomas had made every possible effort for holding his possessions permanently.

Thomas told her an interesting story about the petty Rajah who owned Hansi before him. His passion for sex and extravagance knew no bounds.

"Once he was present at a grand entertainment, hosted by a Mughal prince at Delhi. He became desperately enamoured of a young and beautiful *nautch*-girl, a slave of the prince's wife. Once the function was over, the Hansi Rajah seized the *nautch*-girl and carried her off to Hansi. When some troops from Delhi pursued him, he shut himself up in his house. The soldiers surrounded the house and rendered all resistance hopeless. Rather than yielding the girl, he offered to purchase her for her weight in silver. The bargain was struck, the scales produced, and the maiden was weighed against silver rupees. The ravisher retained his prize."

"It is not surprising that such a man could not defend his possessions against you." Nooro felt proud.

Nooro settled down to a contented married life, though her husband's frequent military expeditions left her distressed, till he returned home, safe.

Gulbadan

Gulbadan was getting old and the ailments of old age started plaguing her. She had developed respiratory troubles. Begum was seriously concerned about her health. Gulbadan was soon bed ridden, and the Begum would periodically sit with her to give her company.

One day Gulbadan said,

"Farzo! I feel that my days are numbered. I want to tell you something about myself. Nur Bai had told me before she died, that I am indeed the daughter of a Brahman. The elderly *mulla* who picked me up and took me to Nur Bai's place, knew my father well. He told Nur Bai that my father was a popular *jyotish*i who was patronised by the then Mughal Emperor Muhammad Shah. Many high nobles of the Mughal court too used to consult him. The *mulla* had seen my father being speared to death and my mother being made a captive."

"Hai Allah!" Begum exclaimed instinctively.

"He realised that the only hope of saving me was to take me

immediately to Nur Bai's *haveli*, as it was close by. He told her that she could bring me up as as a Muslim or pass me onto some Brahman family when everything quietened down. But Nur Bai found me very pretty and decided to keep me with her. She trained me in dance and music. As a kothawali, my religion was irrelevant."

Gulbadan paused for a second, before she went on.

"Farzo, but now I want to request you, that when I die do not bury my body. Cremate it and immerse the ashes in Ganga at Haridwar. I think that will give peace to my father's soul."

"Why do you say such horrible things? I am sure you are going to live long. I shall pray for your good health."

"I want to tell you one more thing. Make up with Zafaryab, he is not mature enough and so is easily led astray. But now that you are firmly back in the saddle, thanks to George, you can afford to forgive him. I am keen to meet Zafaryab, would you please send for him?"

Begum sent a message to Zafaryab telling him that Gulbadan was not well and she had expressed her desire to meet him. There was no fear of harm in Sardhana, she assured him.

When Zafaryab saw Gulbadan, she was in a bad shape. She had difficulty in breathing, and almost choked. After a while she recovered with the help of *tibbi* medicines. She called Zafaryab to her side.

"I knew your father Walter Reinhardt very well. I am your

wellwisher, and so I believe I have a right to advise you on an important matter. Please seek forgiveness from the Begum for your part in the revolt in Sardhana corps. I am sure she is magnanimous enough to forgive you. That will be in the interest of all concerned."

Zafaryab went to the Begum, placed his head at her feet, and in a tone of contrition, begged her forgiveness.

She lifted his face and said:

"I am your amma, it is good that you have come here. You must stay here now, with your family. Bring along Barri Bibi too. We shall make adequate arrangement for your comfortable stay here. You can pursue your passion for writing Urdu poetry."

Zafaryab went to thank Gulbadan, realising that it was her intercession that made the reconciliation so easy.

After Zafaryab had left for Delhi, Gulbadan said to the Begum,

"I do not know the financial status of Zafaryab. In case he needs assistance, do help him."

"Walter had made sufficient provision for Barri Bibi and her son Zafaryab. I too have been helping him from time to time."

Barri Bibi declined the invitation to shift to Sardhana though she thanked the

Begum profusely. Her son, his wife Juliana (Bahu Begum) and their daughter Julia Anne continued to stay at Delhi.

John

Thomas was frequently away on military expeditions to consolidate his territory within Haryana and to ensure regular payment to his treasury. He was very very harsh with defaulters, and therefore, his coffers were always full.

When he was free of his preoccupation with warfare, he would allow adequate rest to his troops. To unwind, he would go on *shikar* in Hansi's neighbourhood. Nooro too would go with him, both riding magnificent chargers. The bush growth around Hansi abounded in *nilgai*, black bucks, rabbits, partridges, wild fowl and ducks near water bodies. Thomas never slaughtered *nilgai*, as some of his troops equated it with cows, which was held sacred by them. He relished partridges and ducks. Sometimes, he would hunt black bucks and had their meat preserved. Nooro too enjoyed *shikar*.

He built a house in Delhi for Nooro. He was always out on military tours; his life was never secure. He didn't want his wife to suffer if some tragedy struck him.

Then, one day Nooro gave Thomas the happy news – she was pregnant. Thomas's joy knew no bounds, and he was already getting anxious about Nooro's health and their baby. Would he be able to manage everything well?

Meanwhile, Marathas grew worried about the ambitions of Thomas and decided to subdue him. Sindhia's General Perron contacted Thomas and advised him to accept employment under Sindhia on very liberal terms. Thomas wanted an independent command but Perron insisted that Thomas would have to serve under him. Thomas refused, and Perron warned him that he would have to face the combined forces of Sindhia and his allies, as Sindhia was not prepared to allow another rival power in Hindustan.

Thomas realised that the Marathas had become apprehensive on learning about his factory for armaments and munitions in Hansi. They also did not approve of his mint, for coining money. He had to be prepared for a relentless military campaign.

He told Nooro about the possibility of a protracted campaign.

"Would you like to go to Sardhana? Then, I will know that you are in safe hands."

Nooro was dying to meet Gulbadan and the Begum, but still she was not very happy to flee to a safer place leaving her husband alone to face the odds. But Thomas was adamant. He gave her fifty thousand rupees and advised her to carry with her all the jewellery, other valuables, personal clothing and shawls to Sardhana.

When Nooro reached Sardhana accompanied by a smart contingent of bodyguards, there was quite a flutter. She first went to see the Begum, who hugged her and enquired,

"Are you happy?"

"Yes."

"Does he treat you well? Are there sufficient number of servants to take care of you?"

"Yes! Yes! *Khala*."

"No, you must call me amma."

Begum Samru kissed Nooro on the cheeks and Nooro burst into tears of joy.

Nooro rushed to see Gulbadan and blurted out.

"Begum has asked me to call her amma."

"I am so happy to hear that Nooro. But tell me, how do you find George Thomas?"

"He loves me and cares for me, what more can I ask for? You cannot imagine how devoted his personal followers and chosen soldiers are to him, which only proves his character. He is frank, generous and humane."

Sindhia's forces attacked Thomas at his fort at Georgegarh, and forced him to vacate. He was able to get away to Hansi, only after suffering severe losses in men and guns. The Marathas offered service to those soldiers of Thomas, who had laid down their arms after the battle at Georgegarh. But they were so much attached to Thomas that they, without exception, rent their clothes in sorrow and said,

"We would rather become beggars than fight against Thomas."

Sindhia chased Thomas and laid a siege to his capital at Hansi. Even the Sikh forces joined the Marathas. Thomas was demoralised and frustrated. To avoid further bloodshed, the French commander sent an emissary to Thomas to negotiate a peace deal and it was agreed that Thomas would be permitted to go free with all his private property including ready cash, provided he quit Maratha territory and moved to the Company's area. George accepted these terms, and Bourquoin, the French officer, who before taking to soldiering was a cook, invited him to a dinner in the evening. There was merry making and drinking, when suddenly Bourquoin called out,

"Let us drink to the success of General Perron's arms."

Thomas got extremely upset and put his hand to his sword.

"It is not due to you, but my own ill fate that my fall is due."

Then drawing his sword, Thomas shouted,

"One Irish sword is still sufficient for a hundred Frenchmen."

Bourquoin had much trouble pacifying Thomas. He agreed to go to the company's territory but wanted to see his wife at Sardhana before moving further on. A battalion of Sindhia escorted him to Sardhana

News of fighting, the slaughter at Georgegarh, and the debacle at Hansi were known to all by now.

George was a broken man when Nooro saw him.

"All my dreams have vanished into thin air."

"What should we do now?"

"I wish to go back to my home country. You must come with me."

"I would love to go with you but in my present condition, I am in no position to travel by land or sea."

"The terms of my surrender require me to leave Sindhia's country. I shall wait for you and our baby, somewhere in the company's territory. Perhaps, I shall stay at Benares where I have a friend, provided the English give me permission."

"I will look forward to join you; I shall inform you as soon as I am in a fit state to undertake the strenuous journey."

Days passed. A bonny baby boy was born to Nooro. Everybody congratulated her on the birth of a son.

"Nooro is lucky, her son will be a great support to her and George Thomas." Gulbadan said to the Begum.

"I am reminded of what the eunuch said when Nooro was born. She had said that I was very lucky that I had a girl. She had said, a boy would have been useless, as we would have to support him whereas the girl would become a dancer and a courtesan and bring wealth to the house. How times have changed."

The Begum sighed.

"Walter was very keen that I produce a son for him. But that was not to be."

"But he had Zafaryab."

"I will be frank. Walter was never fond of Zafaryab as he was a dim wit. In fact, he was so little thought of, that he was not recognised as the nominal chief on the death of his father."

Thomas was not fated to see his child and its mother. He died (1801A.D.) of malaria soon after reaching Benares.

In a Christian ceremony, Nooro's child was named John. The Begum decided that Nooro would stay with her till the boy grew up.

Julia

Samru Begum received another sad tidings soon after. Her stepson Zafaryab expired (1802 A.D.) all of a sudden, presumably of a heart attack, at Delhi.

Despite occasional setbacks in their personal relations, Begum was genuinely fond of Zafaryab. He was her closest kin and she was always reminded of Walter, her first husband whenever she met him. She immediately proceeded to Delhi to be with Barri Bibi, in her hour of bereavement and to assure her of her continued support. She was able to persuade her to shift to Sardhana along-with Juliana, the widow of Zafaryab and her twelve-year old daughter, Julia Anne.

Julia was vivacious, chirpy and full of *joie de vivre*. She brought brightness and mirth to Sardhana. She was charmed by John, hardly one year old at the time and would carry him around the house, and play with him in the lawns. Nooro was relieved to have company. She taught Julia how to play chess and the two would while away hours immersed in the game.

Nooro was learning English and practised speaking English with Julia. Both would go out riding ponies in the countryside; Julia was a little aprehensive initially but acquired confidence later on. She started enjoying pony rides so much, that she periodically coaxed Nooro, even when she was not inclined to accompany her.

Julia loved outdoor life. She learnt that one could go boating in the Yamuna. She persuaded Nooro to take her for a boat ride. She asked for permission from the Begum, who deputed one member of her staff to accompany them. There was a dainty pretty temple, close to the eastern bank of the river on a bend, with a series of steps going to the edge of the river, which was called the *ghat*. The Begum's minion hailed a boatman. He had a paddle as well as a long pole.

The water was not clear, but it was quite calm, its surface like murky glass. The boatman rowed upstream towards the middle of the river. There, he settled the boat right at the centre, in line with the spire of the temple, and plunged the pole deep into water till it hit the bottom, and the boat stood still.

The boatman said:

"This temple was built by the Marathas. Sit still for a few moments and watch it intently."

The spire of the temple rose into the sky surrounded by clouds. And the temple's reflection in the water, depicting the dainty slim edifice upside down in the water, complete with the spire and the clouds, presented an ethereal spectacle. It looked as if the temple above the ground was the mirror image of what was in the water.

Julia was absolutely thrilled. When they reached home, she ran upto the Begum and said:

"Granny, I have seen something today, which I am sure, you have never seen."

The Begum smiled.

"Darling, you have to tell me what you saw."

"I have seen two temples, one on the ground and another one in the river."

"So you have seen the reflection in water."

"But it was so magical, I am so happy."

Begum Samru hugged the girl affectionately.

With the arrival of the children the rather toned-down atmosphere of the sprawling mansion became noisy and cheerful. There was laughter everywhere; little John's prattle lightened everyone's heart. Begum Samru experienced a sense of peace and tranquility, which a happy and contented household brought with it.

The Begum observed that Julia resembled Walter in many ways. Her manner of speech, her gestures were all similar to Walter's. The Begum naturally became very fond of Julia and took special care in her upbringing. Sometimes the Begum would take her to Delhi with her, when business of her estate required her to interact with officials of the Empire.

Badshahpur Jharsa, which was granted to Zafaryab as a *jagir*, by the Emperor on the recommendations of the Begum was to lapse to the state with the demise of the grantee. But the Begum was determined to beat the system. She approached the Emperor with a petition; she pleaded,

'The family of the original grantee will be put to severe economic distress if the *jagir* is taken over by the Emperor, it is therefore prayed that the estate be transferred in the name of Begum Samru, step-mother of the deceased.'

She explained that she would administer and manage the estate as she was doing in the lifetime of the original grantee for the benefit of Zafaryab's family including his mother.

Though many officials opposed this proposal, the Emperor granted her request.

Lake

There was fresh trouble brewing up again after some days of peace. Begum Samru went to Gulbadan, her best advisor.

"I have come to seek your advice on an urgent matter. The Maratha administration under Mahadhji's successor, Daulat Rao, is highly ineffective. Daulat is a young man, who is more interested in flying kites, than governance. He has acquired bad company and does not listen to Mahadhji's widows. Maratha treasury is being depleted, as they are not receiving any revenues. I have information that Zaman Shah, the Afghan King, son of Ahmad Shah Durrani, victor of third battle of Panipat, is planning to invade our country. Even the Emperor is likely to welcome him, as he is now sick of the poor administration of the Sindhia. I am an ally of the Sindhia, so my position has become complicated, especially because the Marathas tremble with fear at the very prospect of having to fight the Afghans. I cannot figure out, as to what I should do to secure my *jagir* and my corps."

Gulbadan thought over it.

"I doubt if Zaman Shah can cross the Punjab; the Sikhs will act as a strong barrier. The situation is very different now, than it was in his father's time. Any way, from what you say, I am sure the Company's army will be the main beneficiary of these developments. I feel we should arrive at some understanding with the British to protect our interests."

At that time, Samru's battalions had been sent to the Deccan to supplement the Maratha army in their fight against Company's forces. Though the Begum agreed with the prognosis of Gulbadan, she was not clear how she should proceed to befriend the British. Ultimately, she asked one of her confidants Mir Muhammad Jafar to sound out the company's agent, located at Bareilly at that time. It so happened that the company too was keen to forge new alliances in view of the impending storm. To earn the goodwill of the company's forces, Begum recalled her battalions from the Deccan and initiated steps to befriend the Company's general.

Not long after, the Maratha forces commanded by General Perron and the Company's army met at the decisive battle of Patpargunj. Despite their gallantry and heroic deeds, Sindhia's forces suffered severe reverses and the control of Delhi as well as that of the king, passed into English hands. (1803 A.D.) Prior to the battle for Delhi, the English were worried that the Marathas might spirit Shah Alam away to some secure place, as he was the symbol of sovereignty of Hindustan. They had taken steps to prevent such an eventuality with the help of disgruntled elements of the Mughal court.

The brilliant success of the British arms brought to the Begum's mind the words of Walter. He had cautioned her that the English might try to take revenge on her as they had failed to punish him for the crimes, which they attributed to him. She decided to make an immediate overture to Lord Lake, the commander of the victorious forces in person. Decked up in all her regalia, and armed with her skills learnt as a courtesan, she arrived at the headquarters of the general just after dinner, carried in her palanquin right upto the reception tent. His lordship came out to receive her.

Having enjoyed his drinks and dinner, his lordship was in a happy state of mind and was absolutely bewitched by his charming visitor. He gallantly advanced towards her and took her in his arms and planted warm kisses on her lips, much to the dismay of his attendants and those of the Begum. Samru Begum felt a flutter in her heart but controlled herself. She still had a weakness for smart Europeans!

The Begum could not get over her apprehensions about future and decided to have an early treaty with the English commander. She also set about holding consultations with other chiefs in the region, specially the Sikhs on the West of Yamuna, who were all assiduously playing upon her fears.

'You cannot trust the English. They will show their true colours once they have consolidated their military position.'

Lord Lake appointed Colonel Ochterlony as Resident of the Honourable Company at the Mughal Emperor's court and then proceeded to Agra to capture the fort there. While he was on his way, an agent of the Begum caught up with him and submitted proposals on her behalf for a treaty. His Lordship immediately sent him back directing the agent to advise her Highness to stand fast and not to move from Sardhana.

The Agra fort fell to him after a brief fight and he discovered an amount of rupees twenty-eight lakhs (twenty-eight hundred thousand) in cash, in the fort treasury. He distributed the entire amount as prize money between his officers and soldiers. The Governor-General was highly critical of Lord Lake's gesture. The incident sent shock waves throughout Hindustan. The word 'prize-money' came to acquire notoriety and the English came to be widely identified as greedy and unjust. Begum Samru was frightened and became even more worried about her *jagir*.

Ochterlony

The Begum was determined to safeguard her interests in all possible ways. She decided to cultivate, socially, the civil and military officers of the company.

She went to see the *mallika*.

"Now that the English have become rulers of Hindustan, it is essential for some one to forge close contacts with the English officers based here, on behalf of his Majesty, in the interests of the king and his kingdom. I think I can perform that role . I have been learning the English language so that I can communicate directly with the English elite without the intrusion of an interpreter. I have been practising speaking English with a few missionaries. Nobody in the Red Fort has any knowledge of the English language.

But for this purpose, I have to have a decent residence in keeping with my dignity, which should suitably impress the English, whether based here or passing through Delhi. I shall hold parties for the English and entertain them. But I have no suitable piece of land here. I have to request that you may please recommend to his Majesty to grant to me a suitable plot of land, at a good location."

"His Majesty is now almost an invalid. He is after all about eighty years old. He leaves most of the work to Akbar, I shall talk to him in the first instance."

Samru Begum was keen to call on Ochterlony and congratulate him on his appointment as Resident. Before going to see him, she collected all available details about him. She learnt that he was quite a colourful individual who lived like a *nabob*. He had many concubines and had fathered many children as well. He smoked a hookah like her. He was about forty-five years old at that time.

She sought an appointment with the Resident and took a substantial quantity of superior tobacco for him. As soon as she entered his office, he stood up and said rather effusively:

"Your highness, you are most welcome."

She presented him the box of tobacco.

"Congratulations on your appointment as the first Resident at Delhi, after the English victory."

"Lord Lake talked to me about you. We will have a lot to talk to each other. Do remain in touch with me."

Begum Samru was satisfied with her first encounter with Ochterlony and concluded that she can do business with him.

On her return to Sardhana, she learnt that her fears were well founded and Walter's dying anxiety had come to pass.

Once after the control of Delhi passed into English hands, the Governor-General issued instructions to Lord Lake:

'Commute the Begum's *jagir* for a suitable stipend, the extent of which must be regulated by the profits which she actually derives from her territorial possessions.'

These developments caused acute distress to the Begum. She represented to the Governor-General against these instructions who relented a little. He modified his earlier orders but still insisted on her vacating Sardhana, in exchange for another area West of the river Yamuna. Further, she was advised to see the Resident.

When she saw the Resident in mid-November of 1803, she was offered an alternative site on life-long lease. She was determined to continue to retain her existing assets. She explained to Ochterlony:

"Do you, my brother, come and having laid hold of my hand, turn me out of my abode? The world is not small and I am not lame. I will sit down in some corner and pass my time in solitude."

"The British Government means no harm. For long- term political reasons, it is considered essential to move you to some other, equally good location."

"I have spent lakhs of rupees in buildings and dwellings. There are near a thousand destitute persons and lame and blind people in my territory, for whom I have constructed abodes with my own money. I could never imagine, that as a person with the same faith as the Britishers, I would be treated so harshly. I request that you pay us a visit and see for yourself, what all we have achieved during the last thirty years since Sardhana came into my possession."

The Resident was tempted to accept Begum's invitation but was not sure how the government would react. He said:

"We will see about my visit to Sardhana later. For the time being, I shall forward the gist of your observations as well as convey your strong feelings to Calcutta. I shall also talk to Lord Lake on the subject."

The matter remained in correspondence for over a year. In the meantime, the Sikhs invaded Saharanpur and captured Guthrie, the Collector, as a hostage. Begum Samru had a good equation with the Sikhs, as she had persuaded Shah Alam to allow the Sikhs to build a few Gurudwaras in Delhi. She was able to negotiate Guthrie's release, paying his captors rupees fifteen thousand, which she subsequently received from the Company.

Lieutenant Colonel Stuart also fell into the Sikh hands. She managed his safe return as well. These events improved her stock with the Company's officials.

After much wrangling, the Company gave Samru Begum absolute life-time right over the *jagir* of Sardhana in August 1805, two years after their control of the Mughal king of Delhi. She was allowed to retain her corps, with the understanding that her troops would be at the disposal of the British forces in

Hindustan.

The Begum, of course, realised that Ochterlony had been very helpful in getting a favourable decision for her. She promptly expressed her gratitude.

"I am grateful to you for your help in the matter. Now you must pay us a visit to Sardhana. Such a visit will enable you to see for yourself our achievements in various spheres."

Samru Begum realised that with his lifestyle, Ochterlony must be short of cash. She hoped to help him out on an opportune occasion.

The Resident accepted the Begum's invitation, and with his young nephew Alfred Dyce, visited Sardhana on a weekend.

The Resident observed that the fields looked greener and more flourishing than in neighbouring territories. The people appeared happier and more prosperous. The Resident was impressed and rather surprised at the excellent management of her estate.

The visitors were extended royal treatment. The Begum laid on lavish dinners and served imported wines. They were introduced to all the family members, including the children.

The young Alfred Dyce was astonished at the royal lifestyle of the Begum. He was more than bowled over by the 16 year old vivacious Julia Ann. She, in her usual exhubrent style, dragged Alfred saying,

"You must come with me to the lawn outside, I will show a

sight, you may not have seen earlier."

Seeing them go out, little John followed them, toddling slowly with his nanny in tow. Julia said loudly to John,

'Walk fast, you old man. We have work for you.'

She guided Alfred to the far corner of the lawn, where a short tree stood, laden with honey scented white petite flowers of harsingar.

Julia pointed to the small petals of harsingar wafting down in the breeze, forming a white bed under the tree. Alfred said,

"This is wonderful. They look like tiny snow flakes!"

Julia asked John to gather the petals from the ground. Excitedly, he went about gathering as much as he could with his chubby hands. Soon, there was a small heap. The petals continued to fall down. Julia put the gathered petals into a basket, and all of them trooped inside with it.

After spending an enjoyable weekend at Sardhana, Ochterlony decided to leave. Julia said to him:

"Sir, extend your stay a little more; I shall take Alfred for boating."

"Darling I have lot of work to do."

While leaving, Ochterlony said to the Begum,

"You have a loveable grand daughter."

Ultimate Peace

Shah Alam was a pathetic sightless figure. The Begum was genuinely fond of the king, and used to regularly visit the Red Fort.

"I hear that His Majesty is so fond of Prince Akbar that he makes him sleep in his chamber. Is that so?" One day the Begum asked the queen.

"He used to insist on that, but no longer. After all, Akbar himself is nearing fortyfive. But the Emperor, still wants Akbar to eat with him from the same dish."

The King was very happy to have Zebun-Nissa near him. Whenever she visisted the royal couple, the King would say:

"Bring her near me, let me touch her."

When she went to him, he would say,

"Zebun-Nissa, hold my hands. Your company gives me solace. I am not going to last for long. What a miserable life has this king been blessed with! I am now looking forward to the ultimate peace."

Once he said:

"I have asked Akbar to treat you like a sister when he becomes the King, though I have a feeling that he would need your support, rather than the other way."

Shah Alam expired in 1806, at the age of eighty-three. Begum Samru rushed to Delhi to offer condolences to the bereaved queen. The widowed queen said:

"As the end came near, he asked me to read out the elegy he had written many years earlier when he was blinded. When I started reading, he listened intently and stopped me when I reached the lines:

Learn that imperial pride, and star-clad power,

Are but the fleeting pageants of an hour;

In the true crucible of dire distress,

Purged of alloy, thy sorrows soon shall cease;

The Begum burst into tears.

As she was leaving, Akbar Shah's mother, the *mallika* said,

"I have asked Akbar to give you a good piece of land in Delhi, when he becomes the King."

Soon after Akbar assumed the title of King in 1806 and *khutba* was read from Jama masjid in his name, he granted the garden, called *khas mahal* including its extensive lands to Zebun-Nissa. She had rendered many valuable services to the house of Taimur, and had personally extricated Shah Alam, the late Emperor, from precarious situations on at least two occasions.

Khas mahal was situated close to the Red Fort, abutting the Chandni Chowk and was full of cypress trees. It also had a pavillion in the Mughal style. Samru Begum immediately set about planning and building a magnificent palace for herself in this land. She was keen to be phyically close to the centre of British power. She was no longer anxious about her *jagir* and her corps, yet she wanted to weild her clout with the new rulers to the maximum possible extent.

Within a short period, a magnificent palace came up, which became an important landmark of Delhi. The mansion stood in imposing aloofness, in the midst of a huge and tastefully laid out garden. There was a large hall with exquisite parquet flooring that served as a ballroom for the European gentry. The main palace was approached by a cypress-lined drive, taking off from Chandni Chowk. The visitors got down from their carriages at the foot of a massive stairway.

When the mansion was completed, all her dependants including Gulbadan came to Delhi to see the palace. Barri Bibi said to Begum Samru:

"Your mansion is the most impressive palace in Delhi. The royal residence within the Red Fort has history behind it, but it is out of date and is too spread out. I am sure Walter, in heaven, would be very happy at your achievements."

Gulbadan and Samru Begum went to the top of the building. She stood on the roof of her palace, and tried to find out Nur Bai's haveli, which was only a mile away. She asked

Gulbadan if she could identify it. Numerous buildings obstructed the view of her old abode. But the domes of Jama Masjid were visible. Gulbadan said:

"You had come to Nur Bai's haveli as Farzana, more than four decades ago. Who could have imagined then that you would one day make such a huge and beautiful palace for yourself!"

"I would like to see that haveli now."

"It was damaged badly in the earthquake of 1803. There is no one to take care of it now. It must be crumbling. But we can go there, incognito to avoid any embarrassment to you."

The next day both the women, wearing ordinary burqas, hired a palki to Chawri Bazar where the old haveli was located.

On the way when they were near the Urdu Bazar, Gulbadan said:

"I wonder if you ever heard of Miyan Haiga?"

"No."

"He was a dark-complexioned eunuch, who used to dance with perfect grace, every day in the square opposite. A large crowd used to gather to watch him dance. Many respectable people strolled around the bazar just to look at him. They gathered around him, lost in wonder. At times he would sing to the delight of the city folks. At the climax of his dance, the onlookers burst into cheers. At the end of every such performance Miyan Haiga would be a trifle richer."

"I never realised that the eunuchs too could captivate people."

"There have been many wellknown eunuch dancers. There was Sultana who was only twelve year old, but he commanded hefty fees. But later popularity of eunuch dancers fizzled out.'

At Nur Bai's haveli, Samru Begum observed that the neem tree at the entrance had grown enormously, and had twisted and knarled branches. As they found the entrance door open, they went through it. There were signs of decay and dampness everwhere. The roofs of a number of rooms had collapsed. Some poor labourers had occupied the surviving rooms. The place was very filthy. They beat a hasty retreat. Gulbadan said:

"Life is full of surprises. I could never have dreamt that my haveli would be in such a dismal state. But thanks to you, I have had a very comfortable life and I don't need this haveli anymore. I often marvel at you Farzo, how you have risen so high without ever fighting a major war. I sometimes feel that your present success is a reward of good deeds, that is karma, of your previous life."

Even Begum Samru used to wonder, whether anybody could have dreamt of her transformation from a *kothawali* to Zebun-Nissa! She loudly thanked her Lord Christ for his mercies and benevolence.

To celebrate the completion of her palace, she decided to hold a grand function. A massive marquee was stretched across the whole width of the new palace. And from the entrance through the garden, a carpet made of silk and gold was laid.

Brilliant lights were installed. A grand feast was planned.

The chief guests were king Akbar Shah and his family, and the dowager queen. Ochterlony, the Resident, his family and Alfred Dyce were favourite guests of the Begum. In addition, there were senior military and civil officers of the Company Bahadur at the reception.

Alfred Dyce sought out Julia, who looked resplendent in her party dress. Little John was very excited about the festivities and the gaiety. The setting was perfect for Alfred to propose to Julia, who promptly accepted.

After a delectable feast, the guests were entertained by music and *nautch* perfomances by famous artists of the time. Asa Pura, a Hindu dancing girl, was honoured in all the gatherings. Her singing followed the rules and style of great masters.

Akbar Shah was delighted with the party and thanked Zebun-Nissa profusely for the wonderful night.

Samru Begum was pleased when Ochterlony informed her about the proposal of Alfred. She always identified herself with the European elite and the propsed marriage of Julia and Alfred was a fortuitous development, which brought her immense satisfaction. After a few months, they were married in the Begum's new palace.

Ochterlony, the Resident was transferred to the frontier station of Ludhiana on the borders of the Sikh Empire of Ranjit Singh. Seton, from Bareilly, was posted as the new Resident. This gave another opporunity to Samru Begum to throw a lavish party at her new palace again.

To imitate the style of high European dignitaries, Begum decided to have an imposing state coach for herself. She already had fine horses in her stables. A Calcutta firm was ordered to make a high-class coach to be drawn by four horses with two postilions. The builders of the coach did not disappoint the Begum. The carriage was painted a bright yellow with silver mouldings, lined with violet-coloured satin, embroidered all over with silver stars. The coach had window frames of solid silver with the lace and ribbons with silver bullion tassels. The wheels were dark blue, to match the lining. The postlions wore scarlet jackets and caps, almost covered with silver lace.

She mentally compared the earlier coach built by Le Vassoult and felt happy that the new coach was far superior.

About this time, Gulbadan breathed her last, plunging the Begum in deep sorrow. She had been her friend and an associate for over four decades.

Nooro, who was brought up by Gulbadan right from her birth and remained under her tutleage, till her marriage with George Thomas, was heartbroken.

Gulbadan was cremated according to Hindu rites as she had desired. Her ashes were immersed in the Ganga at Haridwar.

The Prize Agent

The Begum wanted to be more close to the privileged among the Britishers stationed at Delhi or passing through, including travellers of some standing. She would host parties for them at her palace. The Resident, in turn, periodically invited her to parties, which other civil and military officers attended.

At one gathering, A.Deare, a lady visiting Delhi, was invited alongwith about thirty other guests. A splendid banquet in the European style was laid on. Begum was seated at the head of the table. After the dinner, the Begum arose and threw over the shoulders of each of the ladies, a wreath of flowers of tuberose, woven together on a narrow gold ribbon.

Two folding doors of the saloon flew open as if by enchantment to the strains of soft music. A number of young girls in pretty dresses with strings of bells strung round their ankles appeared on the doorway. They commenced their dancing by jingling the bells in unison with the notes of the musical instruments. They swayed together with perfect grace, their bodies moving slowly, their eyes turned towards heaven.

One item of the *nautch* was a performance by three girls who related a tale by different gestures, which the guests could follow easily. One dancer, more superbly dressed than the others, came forward alone to go through the motions of flying a kite. This item impressed the guests so much that they all spontaneously stood up and clapped enthusiastically.

A pantomime followed, where an English prize-agent and a peasant from the Agra region were portrayed. The former wore an immense cocked-hat and a sword, the latter was stark naked, with the exception of a most scanty waistcloth.

The prize agent stops and orders peremptorily:

'Give me your jewels and money.'

'I am a starving poverty stricken person. See for yourself, look at my miserable condition.'

The Englishman makes a furious speech, well garnished with phrases like God-damned and filthy natives. He, then, takes out a pair of scissors, seizes the poor wretch, and cuts off his long shaggy tuft of hair close to his skull, crams into his pocket and exits, swearing.

The Begum was well known for her roguish wit.

The pantomime left the English red faced but a point was driven home. It reminded them of what the late Lord Lake did at Agra fort after he captured it in 1803.

A young assistant Resident was rather upset, and out of pique, muttered in the ears of the Englishman sitting next to him:

"A crafty courtesan."

Triumph

As Shah Alam had anticipated, Begum Samru had developed a good rapport with the British officers based at Delhi. Akbar Shah felt very uncomfortable in their company, but the Begum's star was in the ascendant.

The newly appointed Governor-General, Francis Hastings, the second Earl of Moira, paid a visit to Delhi. He ignored Shah Akbar, the Mughal King, as he considered him a mere pensioner of the Company. Ochterlony had suitably briefed the Governor-General about Zebun-Nissa. So he visited Begum Samru in her palace. Akbar Shah was quite upset. His queen was furious and believed that the Begum was indulging in some intrigue.

"I told you not to give her that piece of land, the best in Shahjahan Abad outside the Red Fort. But you would not listen to me. The new mansion that she built has turned her head." The queen said.

"But I was under intense pressure from *mallika zamani*."

Akbar Shah's frustration was palpable.

For Begum Samru, it was an ultimate triumph. She realised that her wealth was considerably more than that of the Mughal royal family, specially after they were plundered by Ghulam Qadir 20 years ago. Her corps too was considered more disciplined and effective than the King's troops. Her new palace had won universal acclaim and was said to be superior to the Royal palace. And now, she had attained recognition of her political standing from the paramount power. It seemed that she had surpassed the King in importance.

It was not only the nominal King of Delhi who felt slighted, but even the Rajahs and chiefs in Hindustan were taken aback.

The Governor-General sent an invitation to the Begum to dine with him at his Delhi residence. Hastings had evidently been greatly impressed by the old Begum. She had the gift of gab and was an excellent raconteur. The two enjoyed each other's company. Hastings enjoyed his drink and was known to lose control occasionally. He was so fascinated by the Beugm that they continued their conversation late into the night.

Hastings was anxious to learn about her assessment of the security risks to the Company's territories. The danger from the Afghans and the question of fidelity of Ranjit Singh, the Sikh ruler of the Punjab, weighed heavily on his mind. He got information from her about the Jat Rajah of Bharatpur and the Rajput states. He was eager to learn about the Jat Kingdom, as it was the only state, which was able to repel Lord Lake's invasion. Not surprisingly, the Jat Rajah had become quite haughty after his success.

Goernor-General wished to visit Agra and requested the Begum to accompany him. He felt that she could help in breaking the ice between the Jat Rajah and the British authorities. At Agra too, the two got along famously. It seemed they never got tired of each other's company.

The Begum told him about her conversion to Christian faith in 1781. As Revd. Fr Gregorio, a Carmelite monk who had baptized her, was still in Agra, she suggested to Hastings that she could invite him for dinner if he had no objection. The Governor-General welcomed the suggestion, as he wanted to learn about the progress on the conversion front.

Hastings took the opportunity to open the dialogue at the dining table:

"Considering the ease with which you baptized Begum Samru, I presume you are quite successful in getting a large number of followers."

"I am afraid our progress in that direction, is very slow." Father Gregorio said. "The case of her highness is unique. She used to come to the church with her late husband, when it was under renovation. He had contributed handsomely towards the building fund of the church, the site for which, was gifted by the great Emperor Akbar, more than 250 years ago."

Gregorio turned to look at the Begum, and smiled.

"Her highness was a genuine and voluntary convert to our

faith, we made very little effort in the matter."

"Why is the progress so poor?" Hastings demanded.

"Because we are not able to communicate effectively with the natives, for want of our knowledge of local languages and dialects. Perhaps few Europeans have mixed more freely with all classes of natives than I have; and yet I feel sadly deficient when I have to discuss anything with them."

"What is the solution, then?"

"We have to learn the local dialects, but the country is so vast, and the languages so many, that it would be difficult for any individual to acquire adequate proficiency in all local languages."

Begum Samru intervened,

"Perhaps it will help if we could teach English to the locals."

"Of course! But that would be a long drawn out affair; as of now even the officers of the Company are so ignorant of the native languages that at times they find themselves in hilarious situations.

I will tell you a true incident, which His Excellency will find rather amusing: During the first campaign against Nepal, a senior officer, in fact, a commander of a regiment had to march through the town of Darbhanga, the capital of the Rajah, who came to pay his respects to the commander. He brought a number of gifts but the commander would not accept any thing. He politely declined to take any of the presents but said, 'I have heard that Darbhanga produced *kauwa*, I should be glad to get some of them.' The officer wanted coffee or *kahwa* but the Rajah thought that he wanted crows as *kauwa* means crow. The Rajah stared, and said certainly they had an abundance of crows in his state, but he thought that they were equally abundant in all parts of the country.

The officer could not still realise the confusion and said that if they could provide a few of these *kauwas*, they would feel really obliged.

In the evening, as the officers, with the commander at their head, were sitting down to dinner, a man came up to announce the Rajah's present. Three large bags were brought in, and the butler opened one of them immediately. He brought out a crow by its legs. The commander immediately saw the mistake and began laughing."

The Governor-General and the Begum too laughed out heartily.

Begum Samru carrying the discussion further, said:

"Under the circumstances, the better option would be to train native missionaries. Please think about it and let me know if I can be of any help in the matter."

Father Gregorio departed, thanking the Begum and the Governor-General profusely. Before leaving, he requested Hastings to visit his church and if possible to attend service though that would not be in the Anglican mode; he further requested Samru to escort His Excellency for the purpose.

Hastings did want to see the church and observe the

Christian community from close quarters; after all the company did want to increase, albeit discreetly, the Christian following in their domains.

In the event, the Governor-General was quite disappointed to see the rather modest structure of the church; having seen some outstanding church buildings, both in England and on the continent. He realised that a lot more would have to be done to construct beautiful and impressive churches in India. He broached the subject with Samru Begum.

"I agree with you completely. I intend to build a majestic church at Sardhana from my own funds."

When they were leaving, Father Gregorio pointed out to the Governor-General, the inscription on the wall of the inner arch, which stated that the cost of renovation and changes of the church building were met by the generosity of Signor Walter Reinhardt Sombre.

The Governor-General was concerned with the attitude of the Jat Rajah of Bharatpur, who had not responded to the gestures from the British authorities. He wanted the Begum to act as a facilitator. She requested the Jat Rajah to visit Agra for discussions. The Jat Rajah was quite apprehensive of the British intentions, so he expressed his inability to go to Agra; instead he sent a message that he would be happy to welcome them as guests in his capital.

Lord Hastings and Samru Begum went to meet the Rajah and gave him rich presents. The Begum extended an invitation to the Rajah to visit her in her tent. He went to see her, but there was no major development. The Governor-General took his leave and the Rajah went on to Mathura.

Hastings was rather disappointed with the results of his Agra visit.

Twilight

On return to Delhi, Zebun-Nissa went over to the Red Fort to see the *mallika zamani* (dowager queen) and Akbar Shah. As usual the *mallika* was very affectionate.

"Had Shah Alam been alive, he would have been very happy at your success in the diplomatic sphere. You know he used to say that his most beloved daughter Zebun-Nissa would rise very high in life, despite her origin."

She intimated the king on whatever happened. She realized that he was rather cold and indifferent towards her. There was certain peevishness in his tone, perhaps due to jealousy.

The Begum had plenty to talk to her old friend Sir David Ochterlony, who had returned as Resident, to Delhi (1820) for his second stint after a series of postings. Sir David said to her on their first meeting.

"I understand you have developed an excellent equation with the Marquess of Hastings. I marvel at your ability to make friends with people in high positions. You know Lord Lake was always eulogising you."

"It is the kindness of these gentlemen to speak well of me, it shows their greatness to find something worthwhile in this petty *jagirdar*."

On the invitation of the Begum, Ochterlony agreed to visit Sardhana. She requested that Dyce and Julia, and their son David, must also come along with him. David was a ten-year-old handsome boy with curly hair, and was already a great favourite of Samru Begum.

At Sardhana she described in detail to the Resident, all that transpired at Agra and Bharatpur. She related the hilarious tale of the *kauwa* and coffee too, much to the amusement of Ochterlony. She showed him the plan of the church she was to build at Sardhana.

They discussed about the Sikh power, north of river Satluj. Ochterlony told her of the passion of Maharaja Runjeet Singh, the Sikh monarch for horses, specially his favourite mare, called Lailee. He talked of the well-known diamond called Kohi-Noor, which Runjeet Singh had taken from the Afghan Amir by a clever stratagem. After the Sikhs beat the Afghan army, the Afghan Amir had sued for peace. As part of the peace deal, the Sikh monarch demanded the famous diamond from the Afghan, who said that he did not have it, as it had been stolen from him.

Runjeet already knew that the diamond was hidden in the

turban worn by the Afghan. So he said,

'Let us exchange our turbans as a sign of eternal peace and brotherhood, amongst our respective people.'

The Afghan had no option but to comply with the request.

Before the Resident left for Delhi, it was mutually decided that Dyce and family would shift to Sardhana. As Dyce had to periodically move out for his military service, his family would be looked after better at Sardhana. John Thomas, Nooro's son had had grown up into a young man. It was decided that his tutor, Rev.John Chamberlain would educate David too.

John was inducted in the Sardhana corps as as a cadet. A French officer was detailed to ensure proper bringing up of John as a subaltern. Nooro shifted to an independent residence as soon as John Thomas joined Samru's corps. Like Gulbadan, Nooro also enjoyed Urdu ghazals. She was quite contented and happy with her life.

In 1821, Ochterlony, the Resident was again shifted to Rajputana. Henry Middleton, then a collector, was made the acting resident. In 1823, William Fraser was appointed as the acting Resident. As per habit, Samru Begum threw a big party in honour of the new Resident with *nautches* thrown in. After the function, she turned to the acting Resident and said:

"William, you must visit us at Sardhana."

"Madame, the dignity of the office of Resident should not be trifled with. He has to be addressed as 'sir' by all citizens." Came the reply.

Begum Samru was very upset at this snub. She was surprised that a friend of Lord Hastings and an individual so close to Ochterlony, could be treated so shabbily. She thought that his behaviour reflected on his own inadequacies and lack of confidence.

She could not take her mind of this incident even as she hit the bed in the evening. She felt, as Fraser was less than half her age, he had no occasion to feel slighted at her addressing him by his first name. She concluded that her reported proximity to Lord Hastings, the Governor-General might have irked him.

Another incident took place at Delhi soon after, which disturbed her peace of mind. Her elephant failed to kneel down to King Akbar Shah while it passed him when he was on his way to Jama Msjid for Friday prayers. The king took serious umbrage at this lack of courtsey and his displeasure was conveyed to her. She now missed Gulbadan. If she were around, she could have gone to her for solace and advice. In the twilight of her life, she badly needed a confidante.

The Begum felt that the environment at Delhi was no longer as friendly as hitherto. She decided to spend most of her time at Sardhana. She was also involved in the construction of the church, which was her dream-project.

Zebun-Nissa was getting along in years and was well past seventy years. She often wondered as to what would happen to her huge fortune, after she was gone, as she had no heir. She formally adopted Dyce, the grand son of her stepson Zafaryab.

He assumed the full name of David Ochterlony Dyce Sombre.

It was well known that Sardhana would become a part of the Company's territory at her demise and nobody could have any claim on it.

Begum Samru appointed Col. Dyce, David's father, as a manager of the *jagir*. But this gentleman so messed up the affairs that she removed him within a short period and instead put David in his place, much to the consternation of the father of the new appointee. Age had not dimmed her capacity for decisive action.

Drever

In 1883, Begum Samru received an emissary of Maharaja Ranjit Singh the ruler of the Punjab. He made an unusual request on behalf of his king. Ranjit Singh desired that the services of Doctor Drever, then a physician of long standing with the Begum, be made available to him.

The Begum replied,

"I thought that there are already some excellent doctors at Lahore."

"Indeed, your highness, two British doctors, Harvey and Bennet are in attendance on his majesty. But he wants to have the services of doctor Drever too as he has got excellent reports of his work."

"I am very much flattered that his majesty holds my doctor in such high-esteem. But I have to ask Drever before giving you my word."

"I have been authorised by his Majesty to assure. Drever

that very liberal terms will be offered to him and that he would also be appointed Surgeon-General of the Khalsa Army."

"I am not clear as to how his Majesty has suddenly got interested in Drever now."

"I shall relate the rather delicate matters concerning the health of his Majesty. He does not trust the British doctors and was for the last four years looked after by Martin Honiberger, a German doctor. He is a versatile individual. He had travelled extensively before reaching Lahore in 1829. He had served the courts at Cairo. Baghdad, Syria and St. Petersberg. His Majesty became very fond of him. In addition to his duties as a court physician, he was also made responsible for the gun powder and shot factories."

"Rather unusual combination of responsibilities!"

The emissary continued.

"That is not all, another duty entrusted to Honiberger was the supervision of the distillation of a very potent spirit which he invented for the king's special delectation who had lost his taste for ordinary spirit.

"Very interesting!"

The emissary went on to elaborate.

"After four years of stay at Lahore. an overwhelming nostalgia overcame Dr Honiberger so he decided to return to Europe. The king didn't want him to leave, for he had a sincere liking for him. He increased the doctors pay and offered him charge of a district such as General Avitabille enjoyed. The doctor was reported to have told some of his friends that such was his longing to depart, that not even the King's famous diamond Kohi-Noor would have tempted him to stay on."

"I am amazed at the attitude of the doctor."

"His majesty, baulked by the determination of Honiberger to leave, decided to get a replacement. His advisers talked of Drever in glowing terms, they attributed good health of your highness to his medical skill. That is how I am here."

"I am honoured that such a powerful ruler has approached me for something. Let us see how Drever would respond to your proposals.

The Begum sent for doctor Drever, while the emissary was requested to wait in a separate room. She explained the proposal of Maharaja Ranjit Singh to him and said,

"Would you like to go to Lahore?"

"How can I leave when I am needed here?"

"Look! It is in your interest to accept the offer. The Punjab King is a very generous employer. As far as I am concerned I shall obtain another physician from Delhi. In any case your assistant can attend to me."

"Your honour, I am aware of the problems of the Punjab ruler. He drinks harsh spirits rather excessively and indulges in debauchery even when his physique is not in good shape. I understand he expects to prolong his life with my help. He does not trust the British doctors and does not take the medicines prescribed by them. I am afraid I cannot help such a dissolute individual. In any case, I cannot abandon you in your present state."

Samru Begum was amazed at the devotion of her doctor. In the event, Drever was one of the pall-bearers when the Begum gave up the ghost. The Begum rewarded him in her will with a sum of twenty thousand rupees.

In her will, the Begum had set aside Rs. 20,000 as a reward to the loyal doctor.

Final Tribute

Begum Samru now concentrated on causes dear to her. Her fortune was more than adequate for her needs. She decided to put it to good use before it was too late. The excellent church that she was constructing had been completed in 1823. She had assigned a sum of one hundred thousand rupees to provide for its service and repairs.

The discussion about conversions in India she had with Marquess of Hastings and Father Gregorio at Agra had convinced the Begum that a college for training Indian missionaries was a necessity. Begum Samru was instrumental in setting up a college where Roman Catholic priests could be educated to meet local needs. She donated generously to the welfare of the poor, fifty thousand rupees was given to a fund to help the poor of Sardhana and another fifty thousand to the relief of the destitute of Calcutta. She built chapels in Meerut and Delhi.

She sent to Rome one hundred fifty thousand rupees, to be

utilised as a charity fund at the discretion of the Pope. She also gifted fifty thousand rupees to the Archbishop of Canterbury, for charitable purposes.

The church at Agra, where she was baptized also gained from her generosity, when she sent them thirty thousand rupees. To the Catholic missions at Calcutta, Bombay, and Madras she sent one hundred thousand rupees each. An equal amount of money was set aside to provide teachers for the poor of Protestant church in Calcutta. Her largesse to various interests was widely noted and people started wondering about the strength of character of the one time courtesan.

The Begum also started the construction of a massive and magnifient palace at Sardhana. The architect, who had planned and built the church, was assigned the responsibility for its construction. The rooms of the palace were spacious and well proportioned. Sweeping divided stairs upto the main entrance lent added grandeur to the palace. She furnished the new palace with grand European furniture. The new palace was an ideal place for banquets and parties.

Despite her acts of charity and piety, Samru Begum continued to be active in political affairs, which might impinge on her interests. At the seige of Bharatpur, she insisted on accompanying the British Army alongwith her troops, though she was told that the British forces were adequate to meet the military requirements and that she could stay in nearby Mathura. But she asserted:

"Nonsense, if I don't go to Bharatpur, the whole of Hindustan will say that I have become a coward in my old age."

About this time she learnt about the demise of the dowager queen, widow of the late Emperor Shah Alam, who was her great benefactor. She proceeded to the Red Fort to offer condolences. Shah Akbar, the king was in his *tasbeah khana*; he invited her to call upon him there. The queen was also there.

"She was very kind and considerate to me." Begum Samru remembered.

"Yes she was very fond of you; she always talked about the vigorous efforts you made to recover the royal jewellery, rubies, diamonds etc that were plundered from the palace by Ghulam Qadir."

"Yes, we were all very disappointed that we could not restore the Royal jewellery to the queen." The Begum sighed.

In Delhi, the Begum learnt that with the British control of the Mughal capital, there was better law and order there. Trade and business was improving, and there were increasing employment opportunities.

The ancient canal passing through Chandni Chowk, originally constructed by the Iranian engineer Ali Mardan Khan, during the reign of Emperor Shah Jahan had been lying defunct for over one hundred and fifty years. Earl of Moira, the Marquess of Hastings the Governor General ordered its restoration. When water flowed in the canal people of Delhi were so jubilant that they threw garlands of flowers and *laddoos* in the canal as if they were making offerings to some deity. The banks of the canal became popular promenades. Begum Samru rode in her stately coach along the bank of the canal and was impressed by the Governor General's thoughtfulness.

Meanwhile, Awadh was passing through a difficult period, specially after the devastating famine of 1784. Governance had become ineffective. Consequently, artists, artisans, poets and even dancing girls were returning to Delhi.

Begum Samru continued to cultivate the high dignitaries visiting the military station of Meerut close to Sardhana. She had an imposing bungalow at Meerut too. Lord Combermere, the Commander-in-Chief of British forces in India arrived at Meerut in the course of his tour of Northern territories under the control of the Calcutta authorities. Begum promptly extended to the C-in-C, an invitation to a banquet at her new palace, where only the senior most civil and military personages were expected to be present. Even though she was nearing eighty years, she received Lord Combermere personally on the steps of the palace.

The party consisted of sixty guests. The Begum sat at the head of the table, with her splendid hookah by her side; she offered a similar hookah to the C-in-C. At the dinner the Begum was in excellent humour and bandied jokes and compliments with the Commander-in-Chief. But towards the conclusion of the repast, she was worn out.

After the feast was over, a French officer in her service walked round the table and invested each of the guests with a long necklace of pearls.

The guests were entertained by a nautch performance after dinner.

Lord Combermere became an ardent admirer of the lady and became one of her close friends.

She had made a conquest of another English dignitary, in her old age.

Samru Begum was getting increasingly worried about her many employees and various dependents. Despite her bouts of ill health, she was pressing the British authorities to sanction pensions for different individuals including Saleur, the French commander of her corps. Her will had already been drawn.

Begum Samru knew that her life was almost over. Often, she found herself thinking of her childhood. Her childhood was never pleasant, she had seen her mother being ill-treated and harassed by the son of the senior begum of her father. She really wished that her mother could see her rise in life and the wealth she had acquired.

She would often recall the face of Emperor Shah Alam. He had named her Zebun-Nissa – Ornament of her sex, an appellation, which she valued the most. She could not even recall her father's face, but it was the emperor who had called her, 'my most beloved daughter'.

In the mean time, she received an extraordinary letter from Bentinck, the outgoing Governor-General. She would often ask Julia to read loudly that letter. Just about a week before the end, Julia read the letter:

To Her Highness the Begum Sumroo

'My esteemed friend, I cannot leave India without expressing the sincere esteem I entertain for your highness's character. The benevolence of disposition and extensive charity which have endeared you to thousands, have excited in my mind sentiments of the warmest admiration; and I trust that you may yet be preserved for many years, the solace of the orphan and widow, and the sure resource of your numerous dependants.

Tomorrow morning I embark for England; and my prayers and best wishes attend you, and all others who, like you exert themselves for the benefit of people of India.

I remain,

With much consideration,

'Your sincere friend,

W. Bentinck.

Calcutta, March 17th, 1835'

This letter summed up all that the Begum achieved in life. It was the final expression of sincere esteem from the highest dignitary of the land.

Joanna Nobilis Somer Zebun-Nissa Begum, the only Christian chief in whole of Hindustan and the only lady commander of a corps of troops, breathed her last within less than a year of Bentinck's letter.

Glossary

Adab	a formal salutation
Burqa	veil worn by Muslim women
Chaudhrayan	head of an establishment, madame of a brothel
Chapti	lesbian
Deorhi	lobby
Dhow	sea going wooden boat
Diyas	earthen lamps
Eid-ul-Zuha	Muslim festival of sacrifice
Firangi	foreigner
Gau	barrel shaped cushion
Ghazal	an ode, a form of Urdu poetry
Ghat	landing place on a river bank
Haveli	a traditional North Indian mansion
Hindustan	North India, west of Bengal, essentially Gangetic belt
Hookah	hubble bubble
Huzoor	your honour
I'd mubarak	greetings on Muslim festival of Id
Izzat-o-Iqbal	respect and prestige
Jagir	land leased to a grandee for maintenance of troops for service to a ruler
Jagirdar	holder of a jagir

Jama masjid	congregation mosque
Jemadar	subordinate junior commissioned officer
Jhoot	lie
Kanchani	prostitute
Kathakali	a type of Indian classical dance
Khutba	proclamation when a Muslim ruler is crowned
Kotha	a salon where dancing girls entertain also stands for brothel
Kothawali	a woman who works in a kotha
Kotwal	police chief of a town
Laddoo	a popular North Indian sweet meat
Mallika	queen
Mallika zamani	dowager queen
Namaz	Muslim prayer
Nautch	Indian dancing
Nazarana	gold coins offered to a ruler, on being received in audience
Nazir	superintendent of the Emperor's residence
Nikah	engagement as per Islamic law binding on both parties for marriage
Patwari	village revenue record keeper
Shamiana	marquee, an open hall of cloth or canvas supported on bamboo poles

Subah	province
Subedar	junior commissioned officer in the army
Tasbeah khana	personal chaplet for prayer with rosary
Taslim	salutation with the right hand raised to the head
Tawaif	prostitute
Zenana	women's quarters.

References

Dargah Quli Khan	'Murraqqa Delhi' original in Persian (before) 1742 Translated in Urdu by Khaliq Anjum (1993)
Antoine Louis Henri Polier	Shah Alam II and his court (1779)
W. Francklin	The History of the Reign of Shah Aulum (1798
W.H.Sleeman	Rambles and Recollections of an Indian official (1844)
J.Baille Fraser	Military Memoirs of Lt. Col. James Skinner (1856)
Gen. Godfrey Charles Mundy	Pen and Pencil Sketches in India (1858)
Punjab Government	A Gazetteer of Delhi (1883-84)
Punjab Government	District Gazetteer of Rohtak (1910)
Sir J.N.Sircar	Fall of the Mughal Empire' vols III &IV (1941)
S.G.Sardesai	History of the Marathas vol. III
John Lall	Begam Samru (1997)

K.C.Kanda — Mir Taqi Mir, selected poetry (1997)

Khurshid Islam & Ralph Russel — Three Mughal Poets (1978)

Violette Graf (Editor) — Lucknow-Memories of a city (1997)

Ketaki Dushari — A Various Universe - A Study of the Journals

Dyson — and Memoirs of British Men and Women

in the Indian Sub-Continent – 1765-1856 (1978)

H.K.Kaul — HistoricDelhi, an Anthology (1985)

Maheshwar Dayal — Aalam Mein Intekhab Dilli (in Urdu) (1987)

Pavan Varma — Mansions at Dusk (1992)

Stephen P. Blake — Shahjahanabad - The Sovereign City in Mughal India, 1639-1739

Abdul Halim Sharar — Lucknow: The last phase of an Oriental Culture in Urdu

Translated by E.S.Harcourt & Fakhar Hussain (1975)

John Keay	India – A History (2000)
Mohammad Hadi Ruswa	Umrao Jan Ada (A novel in Urdu) (1901)

www.ingramcontent.com/pod-product-compliance
Lightning Source LLC
Chambersburg PA
CBHW051653260626
47170CB00004B/1482